"But we don't love each other."

Wyatt took Laura by the hands. "I know. As far as I'm concerned, it would be a marriage in name only. I'll be able to put you on my insurance so the boys have health care, and you won't have to worry about a job right away. I can help you."

It was a far cry from the last marriage proposal she'd received.

But where had all that romance gotten her?

She was trying to raise twins on her own, and the people who were supposed to be supporting her now wanted to take her children away.

Maybe it made her seem weak, but she would do anything for her sons. She'd had romantic love, and now she was looking at a different kind of love. The one where she put her children first.

And if Cash's parents followed through with their threat to sue for custody?

Laura didn't think she could handle any of this on her own.

She squared her shoulders and looked Wyatt in the eye. "Yes. I'll marry you."

Danica Favorite loves the adventure of living a creative life. She loves to explore the depths of human nature and follow people on the journey to happily-ever-after. Though the journey is often bumpy, those bumps refine imperfect characters as they live the lives God created them for. Oops, that just spoiled the endings of Danica's stories. Then again, getting there is all the fun. Find her at danicafavorite.com.

Books by Danica Favorite

Love Inspired

Shepherd's Creek

Journey to Forgiveness
The Bronc Rider's Twins

Double R Legacy

The Cowboy's Sacrifice
His True Purpose
A True Cowboy
Her Hidden Legacy

Three Sisters Ranch

Her Cowboy Inheritance
The Cowboy's Faith
His Christmas Redemption

Visit the Author Profile page at LoveInspired.com for more titles.

The Bronc Rider's Twins

Danica Favorite

LOVE INSPIRED
INSPIRATIONAL ROMANCE

LOVE INSPIRED®
INSPIRATIONAL ROMANCE

Recycling programs for this product may not exist in your area.

ISBN-13: 978-1-335-58636-0

The Bronc Rider's Twins

For questions and comments about the quality of this book, please contact us at CustomerService@Harlequin.com.

Love Inspired
22 Adelaide St. West, 41st Floor
Toronto, Ontario M5H 4E3, Canada
www.LoveInspired.com

Printed in U.S.A.

Blessed are they that mourn:
for they shall be comforted.
—*Matthew* 5:4

For all those who grieve.

Chapter One

Laura Fisher balanced the crying twins on her lap as she stared at the thug standing in her living room. "I need to feed my babies. They've been napping and they're starving."

As if to prove her point, Garrett let out another loud, plaintive wail.

The thug crossed his arms against his chest. "Just give us our money and we'll be out of here."

She pressed her fingers to her temples. "I told you. I don't know what you're talking about."

Gesturing around the room that had been ransacked, Laura continued, "You have searched my entire house. There's nothing here."

"That husband of yours borrowed fifty

grand from me six weeks ago. I want my money. With interest."

Laura took a deep breath as she cradled the twins closer to her, praying for God's wisdom and protection. "Cash died in a car accident six weeks ago. There has to be some mistake."

Deep in her heart, though, she knew it wasn't a mistake. She'd seen Cash with this man before, at a rodeo, about a year ago. He'd looked like he was threatening Cash, but when Laura asked him about it, Cash told her it was nothing, just a misunderstanding.

What had Cash done?

And why wasn't he here to fix whatever this was? Since her husband's death, Laura had asked herself this question many times. It seemed incredibly unfair that God would take him from her so soon. She already felt lost, trying to raise the twins on her own. He'd promised her that she and their family would always be taken care of, but what she found upon his death were empty bank accounts and a mountain of debt. She'd quit working when she started going through fertility treatments to get pregnant with the twins, because Cash had told her that being there for their family was her most important job. As it was, she had no idea how she was going to pay next month's rent, let alone come up with money for all the other bills, and now this guy wanted fifty thousand dollars.

The thug's partner came out of her bedroom. "Nothing of value here," he said. "He didn't even have the decency to buy her good jewelry. Just cheap costume stuff."

As if to prove his point, he held out her jewelry box and dumped the contents onto the ground.

The first thug looked over at Laura again. "Your husband was one of the top bareback bronc riders in the world. What did he do with all those winnings?"

Laura wanted to ask the same question. But Cash was dead, so she couldn't. Instead, she had two crying babies and a pair of hoods demanding money she didn't have. Cash had always told her he was investing the money for their future, so they had to live lean. Where was that investment for their future?

"I told you—I don't know," she said.

The thug walked up to her, reached out and lifted her chin so she had to look at him. "I believe you," he said. "So what are we going to do about my fifty grand?"

Tears rolled down her face. The babies screamed louder. "I don't know," she said. "I just need some time to figure it out."

He moved his hand from her chin and gently rubbed it over Cody's head. "I don't know if I like that answer."

Laura jerked back, clutching the babies tighter to her. "Leave them alone."

The sound of a truck pulling up to the house drew everyone's attention.

"Expecting visitors?" the thug said.

Laura shook her head. "No. But a lot of people like to check on me to see how I'm doing after Cash's passing."

The punk gestured at the front door. "Get rid of them."

Easier said than done. She'd be going to the door with two screaming babies, and whoever was there was going to want to help her.

"I don't know if I can," she said.

"Do it," the thug ordered.

Balancing the babies as close to her as possible, she went to the door. Not wanting anyone to even get a peek inside the mess these men had caused, she stepped out onto the porch.

Wyatt Nelson, one of Cash's closest friends and rodeo travel buddy, was getting out of his truck. Definitely not someone she could easily get rid of.

Upon seeing her, he practically sprinted to the porch. “What’s wrong?” he asked.

Then he looked around, and noticed the pickup at the side of the house. “What are the Chapman brothers doing here?”

“You know them?” she asked.

He nodded slowly. “Yeah. They’re bad news. Why are they here?”

Laura shook her head slowly. “Please. They told me to get rid of whoever it was. I don’t know what to do.” She tried keeping her voice as steady as possible, hoping that the boys would stop crying as she gently rocked them.

Wyatt muttered something under his breath, then started for the door. “Let me handle this. I know them.”

A thousand questions raced through her head. But right now, the most important thing was to get these thugs out of her home. She’d figure out the rest later. Hopefully, Wyatt could give her some answers.

When Wyatt opened the door, his loud exclamation told her everything was truly as bad as she thought.

“What’s going on here?” Wyatt asked.

The leader turned his attention to Laura. "I told you to get rid of whoever it was, not invite them in."

"Don't talk to her like that," Wyatt said. "Whatever beef you had with Cash does not affect her."

"Someone's got to take care of his debt."

Garrett started screaming again.

Wyatt held his arms out to her. "Give me Cody so you can settle him."

Laura did as she was asked and went to the rocker. Of the two babies, Garrett was the fussiest, and she was grateful Wyatt was here to help.

She rocked Garrett gently, praying that God would help them somehow. She'd spent the past six weeks on her knees, and it seemed like everything just kept getting worse.

"How much does Cash owe you?" Wyatt asked.

The lead thug grinned. "Fifty grand."

The shocked expression on Wyatt's face told her that even one of Cash's closest friends didn't know how bad things were.

"Give me a couple of days, and you'll have your money," Wyatt said. "But I want your assurance that you will never contact Laura or her children again."

The hood held out his hands. "I just want my money."

Laura stared at Wyatt. "What are you doing?"

Wyatt turned to her, giving her a hard look she didn't recognize. "What any man of honor would do. I'd tell these two to get lost, but I know their reputation. They're not going to stop until they get their money, and it's pathetic that they're preying on a widow with two infants to take care of. But it's done."

Then he looked back at the thugs. "I'll meet you at the Sunrise Grill, day after tomorrow, 6:00 p.m. I'll have your money."

The head punk nodded. "Cash always said you were a good man. This is just business."

The destruction of her house didn't feel like just business. And it sure felt personal as the thug kicked the giant teddy bear his partner had shredded just a few minutes earlier. They both stomped out of the house and took off in their pickup truck.

The boys started wailing in unison.

"I'm sorry," Laura said. "They need to eat."

Wyatt gestured at the kitchen. "Do you need help fixing their bottles?"

It was strange that her biggest supporter was, and most help had come from, a man. Oh, sure, people from the church had dropped off meals and things, and Laura greatly appreciated it. But Wyatt had been the one to stop by as often as he could to do things around the house and help her in ways Cash would have. And now he was paying fifty thousand dollars to help her out of this predicament.

This level of help, though, seemed to be above and beyond the call of friendship.

"You don't have to do this," Laura said.

Wyatt shrugged as they both entered the kitchen. "I've helped you with bottles before."

"I meant the money," Laura said. "That's a lot of money."

"I've had some good runs lately. Since I don't have a family, I've been putting most of my winnings away. I might be young in human years, but at thirty-four, I only have a few more years of bronc riding left in me. It's a young man's sport, and my father always taught me how to save, instead of blowing it all."

She finished fixing the bottles, gave one

to Wyatt and settled in another chair with Garrett and his bottle.

"Yes, but if you spend it all paying these guys off, then what will you have left?"

Adjusting the baby in her arms, she continued, "Cash always said he was putting his winnings aside for a rainy day. But there's literally no money. I don't even know how I'm going to pay our rent."

Her sister Abigail and cousin Josie had invited her to stay with them at the family home at Shepherd's Creek stables in Colorado, as had Cash's parents, who lived two hours away in the Dallas area. Cash's parents had been a little more forceful in their offer, saying that Laura couldn't possibly raise twins on her own, and they could give the babies the benefit of a good life. Of the two offers, Laura was most likely to go to Shepherd's Creek, but it broke her heart to think about leaving the home in Texas she and Cash had built together.

Though as she looked around her destroyed home, she wondered if leaving wasn't such a bad idea after all. Was there anything here other than broken dreams and broken promises?

She looked over at Wyatt. "I just don't understand. You two were always duking it out in the rankings, so how can you easily have fifty thousand dollars, and I have a mountain of debt?"

"Cash had a gambling problem," Wyatt said.

Laura stared at him. "What do you mean, he had a gambling problem? How could he have a gambling problem and I not know about it?"

"People with gambling problems don't advertise it. I only knew because I'd seen him get roughed up by the fellows who paid you a visit, the Chapman brothers."

Wyatt shook his head slowly. "That was over a year ago, and Cash told me he took care of it. He told me he was getting help. I didn't have any reason to doubt him. It never occurred to me to look deeper, and now I wish I had."

He gestured around the room. "He was my best friend, and I didn't see it. And now you and the babies have to suffer."

"It's not your responsibility," Laura said. But deep down, she was grateful Wyatt had stepped in. That man had touched her baby.

Her baby. How could Cash have done this to them?

Wyatt looked distraught. “But I knew about the problem. He told me he was going to get help and tell you, and you’d fix it together. And I believed him.”

He adjusted the baby in his lap, then shifted him to burp.

Looking around the room, Wyatt asked, “He really left you no money?”

Laura shook her head. “No. I had just enough to cover last month’s expenses, and that’s it. His parents wanted a big fancy funeral, so they took care of that. All the credit cards are maxed. They were supposed to be just for emergencies, and I owe more than most people owe on their house on our credit cards. There are a few that I didn’t even know about.”

That had been the shocker. Finding out that he had a secret post office box where he was getting a lot of mail he never shared with her. So many credit cards and personal loans.

Until Cash’s death six weeks ago, Laura had thought they’d had the perfect relationship. Her uncle, Big Joe, who had raised her and her sister, had refused to accept her marriage, telling her that nothing good would come of her being married to a worthless cowboy. She'd thought they'd beaten the odds. She'd thought they'd prove everyone wrong. But no. She'd been the one in the wrong. She'd believed in the lies he'd told her. Why couldn't Cash have told her the truth?

"I don't know what I'm going to do," she finally said. Then she outlined the two options presented to her. Both made her feel like a burden, but what else was she supposed to do? There was no money, and she had no job. Even if she got a job tomorrow, she didn't have anyone to watch the babies. Cash's parents lived two hours away, which Cash had always said was a blessing, because his parents had a tendency to be overbearing and smothering. Laura had never gotten along well with her mother-in-law, because the woman always told her how she was doing things wrong. At least with her cousin and sister, Laura would get some level of support.

After she was done sharing her options, Wyatt nodded slowly. "I don't want to see you go, but I think that going home to Shepherd's Creek stables is the best solution."

He pointed at the broken pieces of her

home. "Most of this isn't going to be salvageable. If I were you, I would pack the things that mean something to you, and I can take the rest to the dump."

The dump. That's what ten years of marriage had amounted to. Everything going to the dump. But the truth was, she wasn't sure she wanted any of it anymore. She glanced down at the wedding ring she'd refused to take off her finger. Cash had asked her for her engagement ring, a couple months back, because he wanted to have it reset for her as a gift after having the twins. But so far, she hadn't been able to find the jewelry store that he'd taken it to. Now she realized that he'd probably pawned it, and it was lost to her forever. Good riddance. She pulled the wedding band off her finger and flung it to the floor.

"Was anything about our marriage real?"

Tears streamed down her face again as she cradled her son. That was real. At least she knew that the children were theirs, and they were real.

Cody had fallen asleep after his feeding and was curled up in Wyatt's arms. Probably overwrought and exhausted from the stress of the situation with the thugs. Even Garrett was dozing off between sips of his bottle. Wyatt adjusted the baby in his arms and came over to her.

"Never doubt that Cash loved you. Of all the things I know to be true, that is the one thing I believe to be most true. Everyone who knew him knew you were his world. We'd go out after rodeo, and most of the women didn't even bother flirting with him, because he would always politely turn them down, saying that he had a wonderful woman waiting for him at home."

Others had told her the same thing. But it was so hard to believe that he had loved her when she had so much evidence of just how poorly he had provided for her and the babies.

"This is a big secret to keep from someone you say you love," she said.

Wyatt looked thoughtful for a moment, then observed, "I know this probably doesn't help, but I think he thought he could handle it. That's what he told me before the incident last year. He was always so sure he was going to win the next rodeo and be able to make the money back. And he did. Think of all the championships he'd won, and how much money he made."

His face got somber for a moment, then

he said, "I wish I had been more observant or something. I feel like I failed him as a friend."

Laura felt like she'd failed him as a wife. How could she have not seen?

"It's not your fault," Laura told Wyatt. "Cash's behavior wasn't your responsibility. This is on him. But I'm left to fix it, and fix it, I will."

She was proud of herself, of how tall she stood in this difficult situation, and the fact that her voice hadn't shaken. Though she might have sounded brave, deep inside, she had never been more terrified.

As she looked around at the disaster, she saw the small cross that hung above her back door, unharmed. Her husband had failed her, but the Lord was faithful, and it was time to put her trust in Him instead.

This was all Wyatt's fault. It had been bad enough, knowing he was the one responsible for Cash's death. But seeing the destruction in Laura's home, the fact that these men had dared to come in and threaten Laura and the boys, had crossed a line. And that was on Wyatt as well. He had been the one to introduce these men to Cash. Though he hadn't known back then just how dangerous they were, or the extent of Cash's gambling problem, all of this rested squarely on Wyatt's shoulders. How was he supposed to live with the guilt?

Every day, he sat with his Bible, looking for answers as to what you were supposed to do when your best friend died, and it was all your fault. The best he had been able to come up with was the idea that he should take care of widows and orphans. Which was what he was trying to do, and yet he failed on that, too.

As he looked around the destruction in the kitchen, all he could see was his failure to protect the widow and orphans of the man whose death he'd caused.

Wyatt had known about Cash's gambling problem. He should have confided in Laura, or at least made sure Cash had been telling the truth when he said he got help.

His heart felt heavy at the additional weight. It had been bad enough, living with the guilt and responsibility of Cash's death. But knowing of the problems he'd brought on Laura because of everything made it worse.

No, he didn't literally kill Cash. But he might as well have. On that last ride, Cash had gotten a bump on his head, and while he brushed it off with the typical cowboy toughness, Wyatt had had his doubts. He'd told him that, and even asked Cash to talk to the rodeo doctor. But the doctor had been busy, and Cash had been in a hurry to get back to Laura and the boys.

Every night, when Wyatt tried to sleep, the image of Cash getting in his truck wouldn't leave him alone. He'd asked himself over and over if there was a different way he could have convinced his friend not to get in the truck. And he always woke up, his heart pounding, because not an hour after he'd said goodbye to his friend, Cash had passed out from his head injury at the wheel and crashed.

And now Wyatt had this image to live with as well. The house destroyed, with two screaming children and the terrified woman who didn't know what her future held.

He enfolded the sleeping baby in his arms and kissed the top of his head. "I promise you, I will never let you down again," he said.

Laura turned to him. "What was that?"

She wouldn't like him making promises to her son. She already said she felt like he'd done too much and argued with him over every little thing. But how could he admit to her that he was the reason her life was such a mess? If she cut him out of her life completely, he wouldn't be able to help her.

So instead, he asked, "Have you made any arrangements to leave yet?"

Laura shook her head. "I'd only just made up my mind to go. I suppose, though, I'll need to be out by the end of the month. Surely that will give me enough time to pack up whatever is salvageable and figure out a way to get from Texas to Colorado."

"Don't worry about that part," Wyatt said. "Between me and a couple of the other guys who rodeo with us, we've got trucks and trailers we can use."

The resigned look Laura gave him hurt his heart. "You've already done so much for me. There are a lot of big rodeos coming up, and you can't miss out on them."

Everyone used to always say that Laura was the perfect rodeo wife. She never complained about all the time Cash was gone, and always supported him in the rodeo life. Wyatt used to be envious of that, because he'd never been able to have a relationship withstand the test of his travel.

"It won't hurt to miss out on a rodeo or two," he said. "Besides, Brady has been asking me to come out to the stables to consult with him on a few things."

Brady King ran the Shepherd's Creek stables, and was engaged to Laura's cousin, Josie. Back in the day, Brady, Wyatt and Cash had been thick as thieves. However, while Wyatt and Cash had gone on to pursue careers in rodeo, Brady had stayed at the stables, and focused on being a father.

Just the other day, Brady had asked him if he knew anyone looking for a job because he needed more help around the stables.

And that's when he knew what he had to do. Wyatt pulled out his phone and texted Brady.

Still looking for someone to work the stables? I have a solution for you.

If Wyatt took a job at the stables, he'd be going to Colorado anyway, and Laura would feel less guilty about accepting his help. At least that's what he hoped.

But as he looked at the sadness on her face, he knew she would probably still feel guilty. A woman like Laura didn't deserve all this.

"I don't know about that," Laura said. "My understanding is that you need to do well at these next couple of rodeos to qualify for the world championship. Your last few rides weren't that good. This is your future at stake. Please don't ruin it on our account."

His future wasn't worth having if it meant that Laura and the boys would not be taken care of. He would give everything he had for them. He owed them.

"Like I said, Brady has been needing my help. He's done a lot for me over the years, and this is my chance to repay him."

Fortunately, that was also true. Brady had done so much for Wyatt over the years, that even though Brady had said Wyatt's generous donation to the stables fund-raiser a few months ago made them more than square, writing a check had never felt like enough.

"You're sure it won't be an imposition?" Laura asked.

The baby stirred in Wyatt's arms as he shook his head. "It would be my pleasure," he said.

Then he waved his hand around the room. "Let's see what we can do to put this place to rights. We can lay the boys down in their room."

The distraught expression on Laura's face told him he'd said the wrong thing. "They destroyed that, too."

As she spoke, Wyatt had already started for the boys' room. He hadn't gotten beyond the living room and kitchen to see the damage, but as he did, he felt sick. They had left no stone unturned. Everything in the house had been destroyed.

"Why did they do this?" he asked.

Behind him, Laura said, "They were convinced I was hiding money somewhere. They didn't believe me when I said I had nothing."

To some extent, Wyatt understood their perspective. A bronc rider's career, especially when they had reached the upper echelons like he and Cash had, was always well-known. Announcers at rodeos would gleefully proclaim how much money you'd made that year. Until his death, Cash had been the top rider in the nation.

It was why all the buckle bunnies swarmed them at rodeos. Neither Wyatt nor Cash was the handsomest man around, but a woman looking for a paycheck didn't seem to mind. He'd always thought Cash had been so blessed to find a woman like Laura, who loved him for who he was. As Wyatt entered the babies' room, his stomach hurt at the destruction. Though he knew they were just trying to make a point, the fact of the matter was, the Chapman brothers were just meaner than a bull who'd been spurred too hard.

Funny how those small decisions came back to burn you later. Wyatt had gotten tired of spotting Cash here and there when they were on the road because he'd run out of money. When he said he was pulling out of the world championship because he couldn't afford it, Wyatt hadn't wanted to give him the money, so he'd introduced Cash to the Chapmans, because a friend of his had said they'd helped him out of a tight spot. Why hadn't Wyatt asked more questions back then? He'd chalked it up to the fact that money was tight from the fertility treatments. Cash and Laura were having a hard time having the baby they so desperately wanted, and Cash was constantly whining about how expensive it was.

Cody fussed in his arms. From the smell of things, the little guy needed a new diaper. But looking around the room, he wasn't sure how they were going to accomplish that.

"What's the plan for changing them?" he asked Laura.

He almost wished he hadn't asked, because

the strained expression returned to her face. "We can lay a blanket on the floor for now."

He followed her gaze around the room, noticing that they hadn't left anything undisturbed.

"Have you thought about where they're going to sleep tonight?" he asked.

If only there was a way to get Laura to understand that he was here for her, and it wasn't a burden.

"They hadn't searched the barn yet. I have a couple of porta cribs out there that we were going to use for babies when we traveled. We were just waiting for them to get a little bit older. I've got an air mattress that we used for camping out there as well. I figured it would get us through at least for a couple of nights until I can figure out what to do."

"I'll help you get them changed, then I'll go out and get them." As he looked around the room, he saw that at least a few things could be repaired. "I'll get some tools, too, so we can at least make some of this salvageable. Anything else I should look for?"

Tears flowed down Laura's face as she shook her head. "That would be a huge help. I wasn't sure how I was going to accomplish getting them in here."

She pointed at the bedroom door and said, "We were just coming from town when they arrived, so the boys were sleeping in their car seats. I think that's the only safe place I have to put them right now."

The strain in her voice was almost too much for him to take. She shouldn't have to worry about the safety of her children. At least he could help her make things functional until they had a chance to leave.

"Think about the things you for sure want to take with you, as well as the things you can easily part with. As we clean up, we will sort as we go."

By the look on her face, he wished he hadn't said that. She was still processing the grief of losing a husband, plus financial difficulties, plus having her home destroyed, plus the thought of moving, and here he was asking her which items she could keep and what she could dispose of.

"Sorry," he said, finishing changing the baby. "That's probably insensitive of me. You're dealing with your emotions, and I'm being a guy and trying to push you into making decisions."

Laura had just finished changing Garrett and was cuddling him to her. "No, you're right. As much as I want to draw a bath and have a good cry, I don't have a safe place to leave my babies right now unless I stick them back in their car seats. The end of the month is in three weeks, so I have a lot to do by then."

She looked around at the destruction, then sighed. "Because of what these men did, I won't even get my security deposit back. I truly am destitute."

Then Laura sighed. "I should call the police, but they said they'd hurt the boys if I did."

She looked at him with such trust. "Do you really think you paying them off will get rid of them forever?"

Wyatt took a deep breath. He'd like to think so, but it seemed like he'd been making a lot of promises he couldn't keep. All he wanted was to make up for his sins, but it seemed like no matter what he did, they just kept piling on.

"All the more reason for you to go to Colorado. They won't know to look for you there, and you'll have your family to take care of you. But yes, all these guys want is their money, and I'm giving them that. Still, I will feel much better with that distance between you."

Laura nodded slowly. “It's settled, then. I'll call the landlord and give my notice, and by the end of the month, I'll be living in Colorado with my family.”

“It's going to be okay,” he told her, hoping he hadn't just lied to her again.

Chapter Two

Laura sat with the boys on the floor while she waited for Wyatt to bring back the porta cribs. As she looked around the room, memories flooded over her. Funny how, before the boys were born, they'd received so many blankets, and Laura had laughed that they couldn't possibly need them all. But today, she was grateful for the heavy quilt that she thought she'd never have use for, because it protected the boys from whatever debris was in the carpet.

She'd never have thought that the beautifully framed photos in her home would be a problem, but the men had smashed every single one of them, and with so much broken glass lying about, she wasn't sure how she would keep her children safe. At four months, they weren't yet mobile, but she did notice Garrett rocking back and forth like he was trying to roll over, so she knew it was coming soon.

She left the babies sleeping on the blanket and started picking up the remnants of the bedroom. They'd slashed the mattresses, rendering them useless, but even the crib frames, which obviously had no room to hide money, had been broken. She closed her eyes and remembered how Cash had lovingly put them together. How he'd kissed her baby bump and told her that this was going to be the best baby nursery anyone had ever seen. The little horse pillow that he'd picked up at one of his rodeos that always sat on the rocking chair and gave her a nice backrest when she rocked the babies to sleep had also been shredded. All the drawers in their dresser had been opened and overturned. They'd even taken knives to the two giant stuffed horses Cash said the boys would practice on, because they'd grow up just like their dad. At the time, Laura had thought it was a great idea, because she didn't know any man better than Cash.

Tears rolled down her face and she realized what a joke that had been.

Cody whimpered in his sleep, and Laura looked over at him. At least she had her boys. Cash might have turned out to be a man she didn't even know, but he had left her with these two precious gifts.

Laura went to the dresser that had been tipped over and the drawers dumped out. One of the few things that wasn't broken. She replaced the drawers, then started sorting through the babies' clothes. A shard of glass fell from one of the sleepers, and with a sigh, she realized that she'd have to wash all of this.

Even though this wasn't the task of sorting things to stay and go as Wyatt had suggested, Laura did find comfort in sorting the baby clothes into piles to be washed.

Wyatt entered the bedroom, carrying the two porta cribs. "I'll get these set up for you," he said.

She supposed she should've helped him, but all she could do was watch and cry.

But it didn't take her long to realize the babies would need linens for those beds. Laura wiped the tears from her eyes and went to the closet, where the destruction was still bad, but she saw hope in the little baby outfits left hanging, as well as the stack of blankets that had been untouched.

This wasn't how it was supposed to be.

She brought the bedding to Wyatt, who had just finished getting the second porta crib set up.

When she handed him one of the blankets, he smiled and laughed softly. "I remember this one. Cash had just won the world championship, and this little old lady was waiting for us in the lobby of our hotel. The announcer had said something about him going to be a father the very first day of the rodeo, and this lady said that since she was rooting for Cash, she was going to knit that baby a blanket and give it to him when he won."

Cash had told her that story as well, and they had both been so moved by this woman who had followed his career sitting in the stands, cheering him on and knitting a blanket for his babies.

"I have never seen him so happy," Wyatt said. "I know it's hard to remember the good things about him right now, but the one thing I will believe until my dying day is that Cash loved you and your children with all his heart."

He reached into his pocket and held out the ring she'd flung to the floor. "You might not want this back right now, but some day you're going to wish you had it. If you're not ready to take it back, I can keep it for you."

Laura knew that ring in his hand so well. The inside was inscribed with the lyrics "forever and ever amen," because that's what Cash said their love was. She'd believed it.

But right now, Laura just couldn't. Still, she appreciated the sentiment behind Wyatt's gesture.

"Thank you," she said. "I can't see myself ever wanting it back, but I appreciate the gesture."

Wyatt nodded and shoved the ring back in his pocket.

Then he bent down and picked up Cody. "Let's get these guys laid down so we can get some work done."

They tucked the babies into their temporary beds, and Laura's heart ached as Wyatt took the time to gently stroke each baby and kiss him on the head.

As they exited the room, Wyatt closed the door softly, then turned to Laura, giving her a tender smile.

"It's going to be okay. I know right now, things look bleak. But I promise you, it will all work out."

When he held his arms out to hug her, Laura practically fell into them. She started to cry again, and Wyatt just held her, telling her it would be all right. Though she had thousands of reasons not to trust anyone again, she actually believed him.

Just as the tears subsided, and Laura felt herself relaxing as Wyatt released her, a knock sounded at the door.

Before Laura got to the door to answer it, the door opened, and Cash's mother stepped in.

"Yoo-hoo!"

Within seconds, her face went from a happy grandmother to someone deeply concerned. Laura's stomach sank as she realized what his mother was seeing.

Laura looked over at Wyatt, trying not to panic. Wyatt gave her a smile, and softly said, "It's going to be okay."

Of all people who knew what Cash's parents were like, Wyatt understood the best. Cash's mother and father were always arguing with Cash, trying to get him to stop rodeoing and settle down with a normal job. They blamed Wyatt for being a bad influence on their son, even though the truth was, Cash had been the one to get Wyatt involved.

"Barbara, Mike," Laura said. "It's so nice to see you both. I wasn't expecting you."

"What happened in here?" Barbara asked.

Laura couldn't even think of what the appropriate answer would be.

But then Wyatt said, "A misunderstanding. Some people who had a beef with Cash stopped by, not realizing that Cash was gone. But I straightened things out, and everything is going to be just fine."

"I don't know what that means," Barbara said.

"It's not for you to worry about," Wyatt answered. "As I told you, this has to do with some old enemies of Cash's, but I handled it."

Barbara waved at the room. "This doesn't look handled. This place isn't fit for living. Besides, Cash didn't have enemies. Everyone loved him. What's really going on?"

She wasn't wrong. Until today, Laura would have never believed anyone wanted to harm Cash.

"I'm helping Laura with the situation," Wyatt said. "But as you can see, we do have a mess to clean up, and I know it's been a long drive for the two of you. Did you bring your RV or are you staying at the Bluebird Motel?"

Laura admired Wyatt for how well he dealt with Cash's parents. She was always so nervous around them, because it seemed like every time she opened her mouth to say something, his mother found fault.

"We're at the Bluebird," Cash's father said. "But now I'm thinking we should have brought the RV so we could park here and help Laura out. She appears to be struggling more than we thought."

And there it was again. How many times had she heard them go on and on about poor Laura and how this was all too much for her to handle?

Well, they were right. She couldn't handle this. But how did one handle finding out that their husband had a serious gambling problem and owed a couple of thugs more money than she had any idea how to repay? And that he had left her utterly destitute, despite all of his promises?

"I'm doing the best I can," Laura said quietly.

"Obviously, it's not good enough," Barbara said. "Look at this mess."

She gestured around the room, which looked like a tornado had been through the place. The thugs even punched holes in the walls in a couple of places, asking her if there was money hidden there.

"I'm asking again. What exactly happened here?" Barbara sounded like she was talking to a teenager who'd been caught having a party or something.

"It's as Wyatt said," Laura said. "Honestly, this is all new to me, and I'm still processing. So I would appreciate a little space to figure things out."

Barbara looked down her beak nose at Laura. "But you were his wife. Didn't you know everything?"

She thought she had. Laura swallowed the lump in her throat and said, "Apparently Cash thought he was protecting me from some of his darker secrets. I wish he had confided in me. We would have fixed this together."

That was the most heartbreaking piece of all. Laura had thought she and Cash told each other everything, and they'd always said that together, they could do anything. Why hadn't he shared this with her?

"Aren't you going to offer us something to drink?" Barbara asked. "I just cannot understand what is going on in here. You're being a terrible hostess, your place is such a mess and you're not giving me answers. Mike and I are already concerned about the welfare of our grandchildren, and you're not giving me any reason to feel any better about it."

So that's what this was about. Admittedly, Laura had spent the first couple of days after Cash died wearing the same pajamas and doing her best to take care of her children while she sobbed uncontrollably. Barbara and Mike had arrived during one of those crying sessions. The house had been a mess, then, but it had been a different kind of mess. Since then, Barbara had made comment after comment about whether or not Laura could manage being the single mother to infant twins without their help.

"Laura is doing a fantastic job," Wyatt answered for her. "None of this mess is her fault. She's just picking up the broken pieces of Cash's mistakes."

Unfortunately, that was absolutely the wrong thing to say. According to Barbara, Cash didn't make mistakes. Except for two. He'd made a mistake in marrying Laura, and he'd made a mistake in being a bronc rider. But other than that, he could do no wrong.

"I find that hard to believe," Barbara said, squaring her shoulders and looking disdainfully around the room. "Where are my grandchildren?"

Laura took a deep breath. "They're taking a nap. I would wake them up, but it's been a long day, and they need the rest. Perhaps you could come back later when I've cleaned things up and they're awake."

Barbara lifted her wrist in an exaggerated manner to look at the gold watch Cash had bought her to celebrate winning his first world championship. "This isn't their normal naptime. I thought we agreed that it was best for the boys to be on a strict schedule."

No, Barbara had created a schedule that she told Laura the boys should follow, and Laura had politely told her that she would take it under advisement, then proceeded to raise her sons exactly as she'd seen fit.

"Your schedule does not work for me or my children," Laura said. "I apologize that you've driven all this way for nothing, but as I have asked you repeatedly, I would appreciate a phone call before you come."

Though she knew it was never a good idea to directly contradict Barbara, Laura didn't have it in her right now to appease her mother-in-law when she had so much else on her plate.

"I don't believe I like the tone of your voice," Barbara said.

Laura said a quick prayer for patience and grace, then said, "I apologize if I sounded rude."

Usually apologizing to Barbara was sufficient to calm things down. But this time, Barbara squared her shoulders.

"I would like to see the boys now," she said.

Once again, Laura said a prayer before answering. "I appreciate that, but as I said, they are sleeping, and I do not wish to disturb their naps."

Barbara took a step toward the hallway leading to their room, but Wyatt blocked her. "Laura said they are sleeping," he repeated. "I helped her get them down, and you're not going to spoil our hard work."

Then he turned his attention to Mike. "I know it's been a long drive for you both, coming all this way to see the boys and have them be asleep. But Laura is their mother, and we all need to respect her wishes."

Though Barbara disliked Wyatt as much as she disliked Laura for influencing Cash's life, Mike had always had a soft spot for Wyatt, and referred to him as his second son.

Though he didn't respond verbally, he did put his hand on Barbara's arm, which got her to take a step back.

Laura smiled at her in-laws. "It's been a very stressful day for all of us, with me dealing with this situation, and the two of you having to travel. I'd like to take advantage of the boys' naps to get a few things cleaned up around here. Why don't you and Mike go to your hotel and get settled, and we can meet in town for dinner this evening?"

Barbara looked like she was going to argue, but Mike stepped forward, and said, "That sounds like a good idea. You're both overwrought, and it would be best for us all to take some time to calm down before continuing this conversation. We'll see you at the old town steakhouse at seven."

Barbara looked her up and down, like she was still thinking about how she could get in the last word. That was how it always was. Even if Laura tried standing up to Barbara, Barbara always had a comeback that made Laura the loser.

"Fine," Barbara said. "I'll give you the chance to get things cleaned up around here. Then at dinner, we will discuss arrangements for you and the boys to come live with us.

And if you aren't comfortable living under our roof, that's fine. We're happy to just take the boys."

Before Laura had the chance to even formulate a response to such a ridiculous statement, Barbara and Mike left. Probably for the best, because at this point, Laura wasn't sure there was a polite response to that statement.

She turned and looked at Wyatt. "Did she really just say that she was going to take my boys from me?"

While she understood that Barbara loved her grandchildren and was concerned for them, Laura couldn't fathom why Barbara would have the audacity to suggest Laura would ever give her children up.

Surely it was a panicked reaction to seeing the house in such disarray.

"I'm not going let that happen," Wyatt said. "Clearly Barbara is dealing with a lot of grief over the loss of her only child. It doesn't make what she said to you right. But as I have told you, I'm here for you. We're going to make this work."

Though Laura and Wyatt had always been friends, hearing his strong support touched her in a deeper way. He offered a lot to her today, and though she felt guilty about it, now that her boys were being threatened, she would take whatever help he wanted to give. She couldn't afford pride if it meant taking care of her children.

What had just happened? Even though Wyatt and Laura had just discussed how ridiculous Barbara's words were, he still couldn't believe her offer.

"I know you said moving in with them was an option, but it sounded a little more threatening than that," he said.

The weight on Laura's face made him want to take her in his arms and hug her again. But she was his best friend's widow, and he'd probably already overstepped by holding her too close, too long.

"She asks me on a regular basis when me and the boys are going to come live with them. If I mention anything being hard, or having a bad day, Barbara immediately tells me I can't do this on my own, and that I need help."

On this last rodeo, Cash told him that his mother had questioned him on whether or not it was advisable for him to leave Laura alone with the boys. Though Laura had had some postpartum depression after they were born, she was doing great now, and Cash had spoken glowingly of what a great mother she was, and how having the twins with her was an incredible gift.

He should have realized that with Cash being gone, Barbara would only increase the pressure on Laura.

"Everyone needs a little help sometimes," Wyatt said. "But I'm not sure that Barbara is the one to give it."

Laura nodded. "That's why I'm going to Colorado," she said. Then she glanced around the room. "And I'm not too proud to admit that I'm going to need a lot of help with this."

Wyatt had always loved Laura's fighting spirit. He'd seen everything she and Cash had gone through to get married, to start a life together, to have their babies. She would get through this, too. As long as he could get her to let him help.

"Let's get started," he said. "I know you don't want to feel like you're imposing, but I also know you don't have any money. I'm going to call the trash company and get a dumpster out here, as well as pay for whatever supplies and things you need."

She looked like she was going to argue, except that the reality of not having any money herself immediately hit her.

"Save the receipts so I can pay you back," she said. "And I'm going to repay you what you paid those moneylenders. Even if it's just ten dollars a month, I will give you something."

Though he didn't expect anything from her, and he wasn't going to take her money, he knew that she had to feel like she was contributing somehow.

"All right," he said. "We'll figure out those details later. But for now, let's start getting this place cleaned up."

"I'm going to run into town and get some boxes so we can start packing things that you're taking with you. For now, just start separating things in the piles of keep, throw away and donate. Is there anything else you need while I'm out?"

Laura shook her head. "No. I know you have your own life to live, and I really appreciate that you're here and willing to help."

"I know that if the situation were reversed, Cash would do the same thing for my family."

Then he looked around, his emotions as jumbled as the mess before him. "The truth is, you guys are my family. Since my dad died, I've spent every holiday with the two of you, countless hours on the road with Cash, and I just need to know that you and the boys are happy and healthy. I'll do anything to make that happen."

He pointed toward town. "Anyway, we have a lot to do in not a lot of time to get it done, so I'll be back."

Maybe it made him a coward, but he didn't want to see Laura's reaction to what he'd said. He didn't want to hear how she didn't want to impose or be a burden, or that someday she'd pay him back.

On the way to town, Wyatt passed the local trash company, so he stopped to make arrangements for a dumpster to be brought to the house. Though Wyatt was prepared to repair anything necessary, some of the furniture was damaged too badly to do so. That, and if she was going to live at the stables with her cousin and sister, the house was already furnished, so the only things Laura really needed were her baby gear and anything of sentimental value. It would make the move easier.

His next stop was to get some moving boxes, and he would get enough for both himself and Laura. Wyatt would need to figure out a place to stay when they got to Colorado, but hopefully Brady could help with that.

As he thought of his friend, his phone rang and he noticed it was Brady. Not wanting to reveal too much of Laura's private business, especially because he wasn't sure what Laura had told her family, he tried to keep things as brief as possible.

"What's really going on?" Brady asked when Wyatt was finished.

Busted. He should have known that he wasn't going to be able to get away with keeping it all to himself.

"Most of this is Laura's story to tell, so I will let her tell you and the family when she's ready. But for now, I need to be close to her to help her with the boys. Do I have a job or not?"

Brady laughed. "I can't pay you what you're worth."

Wyatt took a deep breath and said a prayer for guidance before answering. "You know I don't need the money. But this is something I have to do. Can you please help me and make it seem like you needed this favor from me?"

He hated being deceptive, especially when

Laura had been deceived so much. But he didn't know any other way to get Laura to accept his help.

"It's that bad, is it?" Brady asked.

As much as he didn't want Brady to think poorly of the man who'd been their best friend, Brady at least deserved this piece of the truth. "Cash got himself involved with some pretty bad people. I think I have it taken care of, but Laura needs the support of her friends and family now more than ever. You know how prideful she is, so I need to do this in a way that makes her feel like she's not taking my charity when she already feels guilty for doing so."

Brady was quiet for a moment, then he said, "He started gambling again, didn't he?"

"I didn't realize anyone else knew he had a problem," Wyatt said.

"He didn't break his leg doing that bronc riding clinic," Brady said. "But he told me that he'd learned his lesson and he'd never do it again, which was why I helped him out."

Though it pained Wyatt to hear that Cash's problem was worse than anyone had thought, at least he knew Brady understood the importance of his request.

"So you'll help me?" Wyatt asked.

"Yes," he said. "I'll help you. But we're not going to lie to Laura anymore. I regret keeping Cash's secret about his gambling from her. The fact of the matter is, I do need help at the stables, and you're going to work harder than you've ever worked before for wages that are embarrassingly low. Are you good with that?"

There was something freeing about being told that they were not going to lie to Laura anymore. He felt guilty even misleading her, so if this was the price he was going to pay, he'd willingly do so.

"I'm good with that. Next question, do you know of an affordable place I can stay?"

Brady laughed. "I think I can handle that for you as well. There is a caretaker's house on the property that hasn't been regularly used in years, except for storage. I still stay there from time to time when we get a blizzard so I can look after the animals, but that will be your job now, so you can stay there. It's pretty basic, but it will keep you close to Laura and the boys, which is what I think you want anyway."

They talked through the rest of the details, and when Wyatt hung up, he felt good about the situation. Laura would be taken care of, and Wyatt had been given the means to do so.

For his final stop, Wyatt pulled in to the bank. Not only did he have to make arrangements to take care of Cash's debt, but he was also going to make sure that he was financially prepared for whatever was coming.

Laura might not want to take his money, but he would protect her and the boys, no matter what the cost.

Chapter Three

Though Laura had not gotten as much done on the house as she'd hoped while the boys napped, things did look better. Wyatt had dropped off some boxes and moving materials, and she'd gotten quite a few things packed already. She'd also been able to put aside a significant number of items that hadn't been damaged to donate to the local charity.

The kitchen was mostly set to rights, and she had some laundry going to make sure there wasn't any glass in the boys' clothes.

So when she strapped the boys into their car seats, dressed in the cute little cowboy outfits Barbara had bought for them, she was feeling pretty good about herself.

When she'd called her sister, Abigail

was understanding about the situation, and sounded glad that Laura had decided to come home. In a way, Abigail was the closest thing to a mother Laura had. She'd helped raise Josie and Laura when their mothers died, since she was so much older. Not that Laura had told her everything, because it was still unfathomable that Cash had this problem and not told her about it. But at least she had a plan, and everyone there was excited to have them.

She still didn't know how she was going to tell Barbara. That was the one thing she was nervous about, especially since Barbara wanted her to move in with them so badly. But at least this would solve Barbara's concern that Laura didn't have any help. And, if she knew Barbara, Barbara and Mike would probably be moving to Colorado to be near the boys.

After all, that's what they had done when Cash and Laura had gotten married. Technically, Cash could live anywhere as a bareback bronc rider. But he'd chosen to move to Texas to be close to his mentor, Les Rodriguez. Within six months, Cash's parents had also moved. Thankfully, because of Mike's job, they had to stay in the Dallas area, which was two hours from the town of Muddy Hollow, where Cash and Laura lived.

When she got to the restaurant, she saw that Wyatt's truck was already in the parking lot. He hadn't exactly been invited, but she knew that he was there for her, and she had to admit, she was glad. Even though she didn't like accepting his help, having him here would make it easier to tell Cash's parents about her plans.

Today had been a rough day, but having his support had strengthened her.

As she started to get the boys out of her truck, Wyatt jumped over to the other side to undo Garrett's straps.

"I figured you probably needed some help getting them into the restaurant, so I hope you don't mind," he said.

Honestly, it was a relief. Though she was starting to get used to bringing the boys places by herself, it was still a struggle, maneuvering the giant stroller, putting in the car seats and getting everything situated. It had never felt like as much work when she and Cash had done it together, but that was one more thing she was getting used to. Eventually, like many moms of twins, she'd figure out a system of doing it on her own, but for now, having Wyatt here was a blessing.

"I appreciate it, thank you," she said.

Walking into the restaurant with Wyatt by her side, Laura felt a strength she hadn't known since Cash died. Though Wyatt had been part of her life for so long, she hadn't realized how critical he was to her until now. In a way, she felt bad for not seeing that the steady strong force had always been there. She hadn't appreciated him the way she should have, but as she saw him making cute little faces at Garrett, her heart gave a funny little skip as she promised herself that she wouldn't take him for granted ever again.

Since they were the first to arrive, the restaurant staff was gracious in getting them the table in the corner where Laura could park the boys in their stroller so it was out of the way, but still have them within arms' reach.

"Look how big they're getting," Sophia, their server, said. "I've missed seeing them at church."

That was one of the things Laura had let slide since Cash's passing. It took so long to get them ready and out the door by herself to be there on time. It seemed like every Sunday when she tried, something happened to interfere. Like this week, when she'd been so proud of herself, because everyone was ready on time, and then, just as she set Cody in his car seat, he had a major blowout which forced her to not only change him, but she'd ended up having to bathe him it was so bad.

Yes, she knew that this happened to people with babies all the time. But doing it alone felt more overwhelming than she'd imagined.

"You haven't been going to church?" Barbara asked, joining them at the table.

Great. It was bad enough, admitting to herself that she was struggling, but now Barbara would want answers about why they weren't going to church, and Laura wasn't ready to be open with her about it.

"She just lost her husband," Wyatt said. "I can't imagine how difficult it is for her, trying to figure out her life without him."

Sophia gave her a warm smile. "I'm sure it's harder than any of us think. I hope you don't think I was criticizing. I've just missed seeing them in the nursery."

At least some people understood. Because the way Barbara looked at her, she didn't appear to. So strange that this woman who thought the sun rose and set on her son didn't understand how hard it might be to live life without him, especially when it had only been six weeks since he died.

"Thank you," Laura told Sophia. "I have appreciated all of the kindness from everyone at church. I know I still owe some thank you cards for all the meals people brought us, but please know that I am grateful for you all. Hopefully I'll be there on Sunday."

It seemed more important even now, given that they were going away. That would be the hardest part about moving to Colorado, leaving her church family. Though she knew she was going to another good church, because it was the one she'd grown up in and was full of lifelong friends, this place was also special to her.

"I hope so," Sophia said. "What can I get you all to drink?"

Barbara still stood beside the table. "First of all, you can get us a different table. The lighting here is terrible."

Laura groaned. This was one of the reasons she hated dining out with Barbara and Mike. Barbara always found fault with something, and in Laura's opinion, she was way too picky.

"I specifically asked for this table," Laura said. "It gives me room to have the boys in their stroller without being in the way of other diners."

Barbara scowled. "I don't know why you need them in that thing. Are you not capable of caring for your children during a meal?"

How did keeping them in the stroller mean she couldn't care for them?

"They need someplace safe to sit while we eat," Wyatt answered for her. "This place might have the best steaks in Texas, but I still need two hands to cut them up."

Wyatt had a gift for deflecting arguments that Laura wished she possessed. Fortunately, Mike also often played the role of peacekeeper, because he pulled out a chair and gestured at it. "Barbara, sit. There's nothing wrong with this table."

Though Barbara didn't look happy, she sat, and they gave their drink orders to Sophia, who was looking rather uncomfortable by the time she left. If anything, this strengthened Laura's resolve to return home.

Barbara turned her attention to the boys, and after giving them a cursory look, she said, "They look like they lost weight. Are you feeding them enough?"

Then she reached over and took Cody out

of his seat, lifting him high in the air. "Yes. I'm sure of it. He's lost weight."

Barbara set Cody back down, then turned to Laura expectantly. "Are you feeding them according to their schedule?"

After saying a quick prayer for patience, Laura smiled at Barbara. "Actually, we just had a checkup with the pediatrician yesterday. Both boys are growing at the appropriate rate and achieving the milestones as expected. What you may be noticing is the fact that they're growing longer, which is something I've noticed with them. They'll grow out for a couple of weeks, then they grow long. I thought it was funny, but the pediatrician says that's very normal."

Instead of looking reassured, Barbara only appeared angry. "Why didn't you tell me they had a pediatrician's appointment? Perhaps I would have liked to come along. At the very least, you should have called me afterward to tell me everything they said."

Patience. Lots and lots of patience. "I'm sorry," Laura said. "I didn't realize that it was important for you to be there. But I hope you're happy in knowing that the doctor thinks they're doing great."

"I would have liked to have talked to the doctor myself," Barbara said.

What Laura wanted to say was that prior to Cash's death, Barbara had never expressed any concern or desire to be at the boys' doctor's appointments. But at least it gave Laura even more confidence in saying what needed to be said. "If I need help with future appointments, I'll be sure to call you, Barbara."

Which reminded her, she would have to find a new pediatrician for the boys in Colorado. Plus figure out a way to pay for it, since the insurance Cash had gotten for them would be running out soon. More decisions that made her life seem even more complicated.

"And that brings us up to something important I would like to tell you both," Laura said. "As you have mentioned to me constantly, raising twin babies alone is not an easy job. My family has been asking me to come back to Colorado so they can help with the boys. I have accepted their offer, and we'll be moving to Colorado by the end of the month."

Maybe she should have chosen a different time to say it, but there was never going to be a good time. However, Barbara's shriek made her wish she had not chosen a public place to do so.

"How could you do such a thing? Why would you take my grandbabies away from me?"

Wyatt reached over and took Laura's hand and squeezed it. The comforting gesture was exactly what she needed. It was a good reminder that someone had faith in her and in her ability as the boys' mother.

"Since the two of you have your RV, you are welcome to visit anytime. The stables have an RV hookup, and you'll just be across the yard. Unfortunately, Cash made some very bad financial decisions when he was alive, so with his death, we have no money. This is my only option."

"We've been telling you to move in with us," Barbara said. "The boys are the only family we have left, and you want to just take them from us?"

How people dealt with difficult family members without God, Laura didn't know, because it seemed like every second in Barbara's presence required Laura to seek the Lord's assistance.

"I appreciate your offer," Laura said. "But right now, I need the support of my sister and cousin. As I've said, the two of you are welcome anytime. I want you both to be as involved in the boys' lives as possible."

Though Wyatt gave her another encouraging squeeze, Laura's stomach ached at the anger blazing on Barbara's face. She couldn't read Mike's expression, but she hoped he understood why she had to do this.

Barbara reached into her purse and brought out some papers which she put on the table. "You have another option. We had these papers drawn up for you to sign custody of the boys over to us. You say you can't do this on your own, and that Cash supposedly left you destitute. I find that hard to believe, given his success in the rodeo world. You're just making excuses, and I've never been one to buy into that. Take this time to go to Colorado by yourself, get your life in order and when you have proven that you can be a good parent to my grandchildren, you can have them back."

Was she serious? Laura stared at her, then at the papers Barbara had just casually pushed in her direction. Did Barbara really think that Laura would just hand over her children?

"What would have given you the impression that I wouldn't want my children?"

Laura asked, trying to keep her voice calm, despite the way her throat was tightening at the thought.

Barbara glanced at her, then down at the hand Wyatt was still holding. "It's obvious that you have your own priorities. Now that my son is gone and can't ensure that my grandchildren are being properly raised, I feel that it's only right that Mike and I get involved."

Wyatt seemed to also understand Barbara's gaze and what she was insinuating, but he didn't remove his hand from Laura's.

"Cash was my best friend," he said. "I promised him that if anything ever happened to him, I would be there for them. I'm going to help Laura move to Colorado. It's where we all grew up, and we had a wonderful childhood. I know that's the kind of life Cash would have wanted for his boys."

"Cash would have wanted the boys with his family," Barbara said, reaching for Cody.

Before she could pick the baby up, Wyatt was there, pushing the stroller away from Barbara.

"Laura is their mother," Wyatt said, making sure the boys were settled. "And she will be with her family, who will give her the support she needs. Laura has been more than kind and gracious in offering you the chance to be a part of their lives."

Turning his attention to Barbara and Mike, he said, "Laura is not giving you the boys to raise. She is taking them to Colorado as is her right as their mother, and if you would like to be part of their lives, then you will respect her decisions."

Maybe it wasn't right of her to feel this way, but Laura's throat tightened with unshed tears at Wyatt's strong defense of her. Even though Cash had always made it clear that as his wife she came first in his life, he'd also never directly stood up to his parents. Not like this. Cash had always told her to make nice and tell them what they wanted to hear, and then they could do what they wanted later.

But that was Cash. Never directly rocking the boat, putting on the pleasing facade, then doing whatever he wanted.

And in a flash, she understood. This was why Cash never told her about his gambling. Never told her how dire their financial situation was. Just like he didn't ever want to disappoint his parents by telling them the truth and directly standing up to them, he didn't want to hurt her by sharing those hard pieces that he feared might make her think less of him. It broke her heart to realize that her late husband hadn't believed enough in her and their love, that she would have loved him anyway. She would have accepted him, and she would have helped him find a way through it all.

"You have no right to speak to me like that," Barbara said. "You always were a bad influence on Cash, getting him involved in the rodeo nonsense, instead of going to college and having a real career. And if you think that I am going to let my grandchildren grow up under the influence of you and some rodeo queen trash, then you are clearly not as intelligent as Mike gives you credit for."

Laura closed her eyes and squeezed back the tears. When she was younger, she had won the rodeo queen title at a number of events. People like Barbara thought it was just a bunch of nonsense, but they didn't realize how hard a rodeo queen worked and what she had to accomplish to get there. But that was always the default insult Barbara came up with when she was upset with Laura. One more piece of evidence that moving to Colorado was the right thing to do. How could she let her boys be in an environment where Laura wasn't respected? Worse, how could she let her boys grow up in a situation where they were put in the middle of their grandmother's selfish agenda?

"I think we're done here," Laura said. "I wanted to have a nice family dinner so you could spend time with your grandsons, but instead, you're sitting here, insulting both me and Cash's best friend. I know you're grieving and miss him. I miss him, too. But this isn't a healthy way of dealing with grief."

She turned and looked at Wyatt, who was already pulling out his wallet. He selected a couple of hundred dollar bills and threw them on the table. "This should cover what we ordered, plus a generous tip to make up for the inconvenience to the staff."

"You'll be hearing from our lawyer," Barbara said. "I'm sure it will come as no surprise that we will be suing for full custody. A single mom with no income, living in the squalor we saw earlier today, is unfit to raise my grandchildren."

Laura's stomach sank as her chest tightened. Though Barbara had made it clear she didn't approve of Laura as a parent and that she wanted to raise the boys herself, it hadn't occurred to her that she would take it this far. Every time she thought that things couldn't get worse, they did.

Wyatt put his arm around her as he stared at Cash's parents. "You can try," he said. "But as I told you, I promised Cash I would take care of Laura and the boys, and that's what I aim to do. We'll be getting married as soon as possible so that Laura has the protection of both my name and my money. I'm moving to Colorado with them, and until you can treat my future wife with the proper respect, all communication about the boys will go through me."

Laura stared at Wyatt. Had he really just said what she thought he said? She wasn't going to argue with him, not in front of Cash's parents, but this was definitely way more than she could handle. Wyatt turned and pushed the stroller toward the exit.

"Let's go," he said.

As they walked out of the restaurant, Laura's insides were jumbled with emotions. Mostly though, she was in shock at Wyatt's pronouncement. They hadn't even discussed him moving to Colorado permanently, let alone getting married.

When they got to her truck, Wyatt said,

"I'm sorry about that in there. I was just so mad that they could even consider taking away the boys that I blurted the first thing that came to mind."

Then he looked her up and down. "But to be honest, it's not a bad idea. It takes away their arguments about you being able to care for the boys, leaving their only option to prove that you're an unfit mother, and with the kind of mother you are, that's going to be impossible. I can't believe they would even think about putting you in this position."

Laura strapped Garrett into his seat, noticing that Wyatt had already done the same with Cody. That was the thing. He always automatically stepped in to help without being asked. She could do a lot worse than marrying a guy like him.

"But we don't love each other that way," she said.

Then she bit her lip. What if he did feel that way about her? Had she just ruined their friendship?

Wyatt came around the side of the car and took her by the hands. "I know. And I'm not asking for that kind of marriage. As far as I'm concerned, it would be a marriage in name only, other than I'll be around to help you with the boys. This way, you won't be a single mom. I'll be able to put you on my insurance, so the boys have healthcare, and you won't have to worry about trying to find a job right away. I can help you."

It was a far cry from the last marriage proposal she'd received. The romantic one with Cash getting down on one knee after having set up a romantic picnic at their favorite spot. Where he told her about how much he loved her, and how their love story would be so epic that people would base love songs and movies on them.

But where had all that romance gotten her?

She was powerless, trying to raise twins on her own, and the people who were supposed to be supporting her now wanted to take her children away.

Maybe it made her seem weak, but she would do anything for her sons. She'd had romantic love, and now she was looking at a different kind of love. The one where she put her children and their needs first, the kind where she swallowed her pride because it was best for her family. It might not be the kind of epic romance she'd dreamed about as a girl, but as a mother, she'd learned about real love, and sometimes it meant sacrificing all the things you once thought were important to save the ones you truly love.

As much as she hated the idea of being beholden to Wyatt, he'd brought up points she hadn't allowed herself to think about yet. At the doctor's office, she'd asked about options for when their health insurance ran out, and the office staff had given her some pamphlets but told her that she'd probably have to find another doctor for the boys.

And if Cash's parents followed through with their threat to sue for custody?

Laura didn't think she could deal with any of this on her own.

She squared her shoulders and looked Wyatt in the eye. "Yes. I'll marry you."

The next couple of weeks passed in a blur as Wyatt made arrangements to move him, Laura and the boys to Colorado.

Wyatt still couldn't believe that Laura had agreed to his plan, or that he'd come up with it in the first place.

He didn't know where the idea had come from, but ever since it came out of his mouth, he couldn't stop feeling that it was the right thing to do. In all those late nights in various towns as they traveled the country, trying to make a name for themselves, especially after some of their close calls with injuries, that's where his conversations with Cash had gone. Cash asking him to take care of Laura. And then when the boys were on the way, Cash asking him to take care of Laura and the children.

Maybe Cash hadn't intended for him to marry Laura, but right now that seemed like the best way to accomplish Wyatt's promise to take care of them all. He couldn't see any judge giving custody of infant twins to their grandparents when those babies had a good mother. But the Fishers had a great deal of money, and Mike knew a lot of influential people. At the very least, they could make things difficult for Laura for a long time.

Fortunately, they hadn't heard from Cash's parents since the disastrous night in the restaurant. Wyatt assumed it was because they were pursuing legal options, but those options were taking time. He and Laura had already consulted with an attorney, who assured them that the Fishers would have virtually no chance of making their case, given that Laura was a good parent, and that it was extremely difficult for grandparents to get custody over a biological parent.

Still, Wyatt didn't want to take any chances. He and Laura would be getting married once they arrived in Colorado, so Laura would have the support of her family. She and Wyatt had looked into the cost of healthcare for Laura, as well as her other financial needs with the boys, and getting married just made the most sense. She'd shared with him all of the information about Cash's debt, and it had horrified him. There would have been no way for Laura to have paid it back on her own.

Marriage meant that Laura and the boys would have a stable home with enough money in the bank to provide for them. Wyatt might not be as wealthy as the Fishers, but he'd saved and invested most of his winnings over the years, so he had a nice nest egg. It would be enough to ensure Laura had the resources she needed. Plus, even though he'd paid off the Chapmans, and they'd said they were even, he'd sleep better at night knowing he was that much closer to Laura and the boys.

This wasn't about anything romantic, but about what was best for Laura and her sons. Laura was a good woman who deserved all the happiness in the world. He hated that it had been denied her, even more so that the man she loved had misled her in so many ways. Though Wyatt loved Cash like a brother, if he were here, Wyatt would have some harsh words for the man who'd put his wife and children at risk in the way he had.

Should a worthy man appear in Laura's life, Wyatt would gladly step side. However, as he told himself that, a tiny voice inside him asked what he was thinking, and that maybe, given that Laura was absolutely the best woman he'd ever known, he should think about earning her love himself.

Wyatt stopped dead in his tracks. Where had that thought come from? He and Laura were friends, nothing more, and this marriage was only born out of convenience.

Besides, if Laura ever found out that he was the reason Cash was dead, it would ruin their entire friendship. They could never have a real relationship, not when Wyatt had been the one to ruin her life. None of this could make up for the things Wyatt had done, but if it took giving up everything Wyatt had worked for, as well as whatever ideas of romance he had in his head, he would make things right for Laura and the boys, or at least as right as he could.

He pulled up in front of Laura's house, ready to put the last of her household items into his trailer so they could get on the road first thing in the morning. She didn't have to be out for another week, but Wyatt had a rodeo coming up this weekend, and Laura had insisted that he not miss it.

Before he could get out of the truck, Laura was on the porch, carrying a box.

"The boys are sleeping, so I wanted to take advantage," she said.

Laura had been going nonstop since making the decision to move to Colorado, so he hoped that she'd get a chance to rest when she was home with her family.

He helped her load the box into the trailer, which was getting full.

"Who knew we'd have so much stuff, even after what we donated and threw out?" Wyatt said, admiring their efficiency in packing.

Laura smiled at him. "I think we did pretty good, all things considered."

The funny thing about spending all this time with her, getting ready for the move, was that after all these years, they were starting to build a relationship for the two of them. It had always been the three of them, and getting to know Laura on her own was a bit of a surprise.

Like seeing how strong and capable she really was.

When he went into the house, he saw that she'd neatly stacked furniture and boxes, ready to be loaded.

"I told you I'd take care of that," he said.

Laura shrugged. "I know, but I had the time, and it feels good to be useful."

"Thank you," Wyatt said. "I know this isn't the kind of fairy-tale stuff people dream about, but I think you can agree that the most important thing is to do right by the boys."

Laura smiled at him. "I think the fairy tale is overrated. I had that, and my priorities have changed."

"I couldn't agree more," he said.

As much as he'd always thought he wanted romance for himself, he'd had enough of the dating game to know that what Laura and Cash had was rare, and even that wasn't all that it appeared to be. Somehow, basing a marriage on more practical matters felt better to Wyatt.

"Thank you for everything," Laura said, hugging him.

The hug Laura gave him brought a warmth to Wyatt he hadn't expected. He and Laura had hugged hundreds of times over the years, but this felt like they'd reached a new point in their relationship. In a way, he supposed they had. He'd promised his life to this woman, and even though it wasn't a romantic kind of love, it was still a deeper love than anything that had passed between them before.

Maybe this was what love really was. It wasn't about the butterflies or that giddy feeling, but creating a partnership based on mutual interests and something greater than yourself.

Still, as Laura released him from the hug, he couldn't help thinking how she smelled like springtime after a long winter. But just as quickly as that inappropriate thought hit him, he pushed it aside.

Which was a good thing, because as they stepped apart, he noticed the Fishers' RV pulling in to the driveway.

So much for their newfound peace.

The flutter of Laura's eyelids and indrawn breath told him she was saying a quick prayer. One more thing he loved about her. Through all these trials, she was leaning heavily on the Lord, and it strengthened his faith to see how she would be raising the boys trusting in God.

When Barbara got out of the RV, Laura greeted her warmly, as if their last meeting hadn't been wrought with tension.

The lawyer had advised them that even

though the Fishers didn't have a legal leg to stand on in getting custody of the boys, it would look better to the court, if it went that far, for Laura to be as cooperative as possible. Which she'd said she didn't mind doing, because it was never her intention to shut the Fishers out of the their grandchildrens' lives.

And there she was, treating the Fishers with all the grace and kindness that made Wyatt grateful she'd agreed to be his wife.

"You're really leaving," Barbara said, looking at the packed trailer.

Laura smiled. "It's for the best."

A cry from the baby monitor hooked to Laura's hip brought a smile to her face. "Perfect timing. Sounds like they're just waking up from their naps. How about I change them, and I'll bring them out to say hi?"

"I'm perfectly capable of changing a diaper," Barbara said.

"Of course." Only the faintest hint of tension sounded in Laura's voice, but it was enough for Wyatt to follow them into the house.

The babies' room was sparse, with only their porta cribs and a few miscellaneous items they'd need for the evening left.

Garrett was fussing the loudest, so Laura

picked him up first. And, as Wyatt always did when he was around, he grabbed the other baby.

Despite Barbara's insistence that she was capable of changing a diaper, she stood in the doorway and watched. Wyatt and Laura had taken to racing each other to see who could get their baby changed first, though Laura always won.

When Garrett was ready, Laura planted a giant kiss on him, as she always did, then handed him to Barbara. "Say hello to Grandma," she said.

Wyatt held Cody close to him for a moment before Laura took him into her arms. From the way she cuddled him, he could tell that she was nervous, despite her cheerful attitude toward Barbara.

Maybe it was silly of him, but he wasn't going to take his eyes off of Barbara while she had one of the babies in her arms. He already loved the boys, but the more time he spent with them, the deeper in love he fell.

"I hope you don't mind," Laura said. "But all we have are the folding chairs and card table in the kitchen. Why don't we go in there and sit? All I can offer you to drink is some bottled water, so I hope that's okay."

He smiled softly as he realized that this was a stark contrast from Barbara's last visit. True, they had very little to offer, but he was proud of Laura for still trying in the midst of these circumstances.

Mike had hung back and was watching them. Laura smiled at him. "Do you want to hold Cody?"

The delight on the older man's face as he took the baby made Wyatt grin. Not only because Laura had just made Cash's parents very happy, but because of the incredible amount of strength and courage it had taken Laura. How could the Fishers doubt what a good woman Laura was? Wyatt wouldn't have blamed her if she'd told them to leave. And, as she got everyone bottles of water, he could see Laura relaxing as she, too, noticed how happy the Fishers were to be spending time with their grandsons.

"We're hoping to stay here until you leave, so we can have a chance to say goodbye to the boys," Mike said.

At least it would be a short visit. "We leave in the morning," Wyatt told him.

Barbara stopped making funny faces at Garrett and looked up. "So soon? I thought you'd be here until the end of the month."

Laura turned from where she'd started making the boys their bottles. "Our plans changed. Wyatt has a rodeo next weekend, so we want to have time to get settled before he goes."

Even though he'd been willing to skip this one, Laura had insisted that this change in his life affect his rodeo career as little as possible. She'd spent many nights sitting with him and Cash, listening to their dreams of championships. Cash had won it twice. Wyatt was still waiting for his chance. Funny, one of the last conversations Cash and Wyatt had before Cash's last ride was Cash telling him that he thought this was Wyatt's year.

"I would think that after what happened to Cash, you'd give up on the rodeo nonsense," Barbara said.

It had always been rodeo nonsense, according to Barbara. But Laura smiled and handed her Garrett's bottle. "What happened to Cash was a tragic accident. No one realized that he'd had a concussion when he'd gotten into his truck. A bump on the head could happen to any of us, in any circumstance. I support Wyatt and his dreams, just like I supported Cash."

Laura's optimism and easy dismissal of

Cash's death as a tragic accident made Wyatt feel sick. He'd realized Cash could have had a concussion. And he hadn't stopped his friend from getting into the truck and dying.

She would hate him if she ever discovered the truth.

Then Laura handed Mike Cody's bottle. "Anyway, I'm sorry we won't get to spend as much time with you before we go, but this is what works best for us. I believe you have our new address in Colorado, and we can do video chats as much as you want so you don't miss out on the boys' milestones."

"No need for that," Barbara said. "We're coming to Colorado, too. Mike is looking for a job in the area. That's why we brought the RV this time. We'll stay in that for now, and hopefully we'll find a house to buy close to the stables, so we don't miss out on a moment of the boys' lives."

Despite the fact that neither of them wanted to exclude the Fishers from the boys' lives, having them buy a house near the stables would be a disaster. And, from the expression on Laura's face, she knew it, too.

Starting a new life together was about to get even more complicated.

Chapter Four

After all these years, as much as Shepherd's Creek stables had changed, so much of it had stayed the same. Even with a few updates, everything still felt like home to Laura. It was weird to think that the house she grew up in, just on the other side of the paddock, wasn't where she'd be calling home. Instead, Laura was supervising her belongings being moved into the old caretaker's house. When they'd been younger, they'd always been afraid to go near that house. Roger Jenkins had been a cranky old cowboy who didn't want a bunch of noisy kids running around his place. Though he took good care of the stables and the surrounding grounds, the children at the stables were terrified of him.

Which made it strange to have turned one

of the bedrooms into a nursery for her boys. They'd spent the first few nights at the main house while they got everything arranged. Even though Laura had told her cousins not to go to any trouble, when Laura arrived, the caretaker's house had been freshly cleaned, painted and the flooring replaced. She hadn't expected such star treatment, but as she felt the soft carpeting in the master bedroom under her feet, Laura was filled with gratitude. The boys' room was similarly appointed, and it felt good to know they were in a safe, comfortable place.

When her cousin Josie entered the room with an armload of boxes, Laura said, "You really didn't have to go to all this trouble."

Josie set the boxes down and gave her a hug. "Yes, we did. The house hadn't been lived in for years, and there were a lot of things that needed to be repaired and replaced. Even if we hadn't done it for you, we would have had to do it for whoever took the caretaker's job Brady was hiring for."

Laura gave her cousin a skeptical look. "So that job was real? Brady didn't just hire Wyatt to help me out?"

Josie shook her head. "Trust me, the job is real. With the expansion of the stables to work in conjunction with the rec center for their programs, we have a lot more business coming in. But with that, we have more to do around here to make sure we're adhering to safety standards for the recreation program. It's too much for us to do on our own, so we've been actively looking for assistance. Having Wyatt here is going to be a huge blessing to us."

Taking a deep breath, Laura told herself she needed to accept this blessing. This was what families did, and after years of only having video chats with her sister, and now a few months with her cousin, Laura had to get used to the idea of having the support of a family again. Though Josie and Abigail had gone to all this effort, it didn't feel as intrusive as when Barbara took over. The women had asked her opinion on colors and done their best to make it feel like Laura's home, not theirs, and not what they thought Laura really wanted.

Not all help from family came with strings.

As if she knew Laura was thinking about her, Barbara entered the room, the familiar look of disdain on her face. "This is much smaller than your other house. Are you sure there's going to be room for everyone?"

Not this again. True, it was half the size of their old house, but Laura had always thought that it was just a little too big. It certainly wasn't the mansion Barbara and Mike lived in, but she didn't need something so fancy. That was what Barbara had never understood. Laura didn't want or need luxury. She just needed to be surrounded by the people she loved.

Laura gestured around the room, then out the door. "The living room is plenty big for us to spend time in, as well as have all the boys' things. The kitchen is well appointed, and it actually has more storage space than I had at the other house."

Barbara gave a slight sniff. "There are only three bedrooms. You've said that one is for the boys, one is for you and Wyatt, and the other Wyatt needs for his office. Where will we stay?"

It was funny that Barbara made this argument now, considering that when Cash was alive, they never stayed at the house. They either used the RV or booked a room at the local motel. Having them here would be way too stressful. What Barbara didn't know, and Laura wasn't going to tell her or anyone else, was that the room they were calling Wyatt's office was actually his bedroom. Although they hadn't had the ceremony yet, Laura and Wyatt had agreed that while their marriage would be in name only, no one else had to know that.

Especially not Barbara, since nothing ever satisfied her.

"You've always been happy staying in a motel or your RV," Laura said smoothly, pointing at the door. "Why don't we go sit for a while?"

Everyone shuffled into the living room, where it was beginning to look like home.

Wyatt entered the house, nodding at something Brady said. It was good to see the two old friends back together again, but a pang hit Laura's heart, knowing that Cash wasn't here. That was the funny thing about grief. Just when she thought she was okay, she still had moments like these where she thought about Cash and how much she missed him. But those thoughts were always replaced by the sense of betrayal she felt, knowing what Cash had done. At some point, she would have to forgive him, and someday, she would. But as she watched Barbara move the couch for the second time since they'd brought it in, Laura was filled with fury at the position her husband had put her in.

"Why are you moving that?" Wyatt asked. "Laura and I agreed that it was going to stay there, because it gave more floor space for the boys to roam around."

Hadn't Laura told her that very thing? It was maddening to constantly fight these battles with Barbara.

"Yes, but once the boys start climbing, they can climb on the couch and with it right next to the window, they're liable to fall out and hurt themselves," Barbara said.

"That set of windows is painted shut," Josie said. "Trust me, we tried everything, because when we were repainting in here, we could have used some fresh air."

Instead of those words appeasing Barbara, she glared at Josie. "Did you check to make sure that these were low-chemical paints? Too many chemicals are bad for their development and can hurt their cognitive growth."

Josie gave Laura a look as if to say, "You were not kidding about her," then smiled at Barbara. "Absolutely. It's very important to me to be as environmentally friendly and use as minimal chemicals as humanly possible."

The men pushed the couch back into place

and flopped down on it. "I think we finally got everything," Brady said.

Barbara still didn't look satisfied. "It seems like a fire hazard to have the boys in a room where the windows don't open."

Was anything going to ever be good enough for Barbara?

Before Laura could answer, Josie said, "Because of our status working with the rec center, we made sure every building meets or exceeds fire code. While that particular set of windows doesn't open, they're near enough to the front door that there's still a good exit from this room. If you like, I can show you all the ways the house is prepared for fire safety, as I'm getting ready for the fire marshal to come out in a couple of weeks to do their quarterly inspection."

Barbara looked like she wanted to retort, but didn't know what to say. Laura felt herself relax a little more as she realized that her cousin had her back. All these years, Laura had put up with Barbara's nonsense, and Cash would tell her to do what was necessary to keep the peace until their visit with his mother was over. But more and more, she was questioning if Cash had been right to do so. It would have meant so much to her if he'd only stood up to Barbara on Laura's behalf the way Josie was now.

The way Wyatt had been.

She looked over at the handsome cowboy who'd been her champion. Maybe they didn't have the romantic kind of love she'd thought she'd had with Cash, but the friendship and mutual respect Laura and Wyatt had counted for a lot.

As if he knew that Laura's nerves were already fried, Garrett let out a wail from the bedroom. They'd gotten the twins' bedroom set up as quickly as possible so they boys had a place to be safe and out of the commotion. Laura had just laid the boys down for a nap a short time ago. She'd been counting on them sleeping for at least another hour.

"I'll get him," Barbara said.

Laura was going to argue, but Wyatt put his hand on her arm. "That would be great, thank you," Wyatt said. "After all, you're here to spend time with your grandchildren, not help us unpack."

Hopefully Barbara didn't find fault with anything in the boys' room because Laura feared that it would only solidify Barbara's opinion that Laura was an incompetent mother. It seemed to be how Laura felt every time Barbara was near. But she couldn't deny the look of happiness on Barbara's face when she went into the boys' room.

Wyatt gestured at the recliner in the corner. "Now you sit. Don't think I haven't noticed that you've been on your feet all day. When we stopped for lunch, you kept working."

Laura sat in the recliner and let out a long sigh. "I wanted to take advantage of having everybody oohing and ahhing over the babies so I could get something done."

Wyatt grinned. "And now you're going to get to take advantage of having Barbara's help and get a little rest. In fact, I think that we're just going to order pizza for dinner tonight, instead of you having to think of making something."

Laura gestured at the kitchen. "No need. One of the ladies from church already brought over some kind of casserole. We just have to stick it in the oven."

Although Laura had loved her old church in Texas, moving back to Shepherd's Creek and having the community already surround them with so much love reaffirmed her decision to come home. They'd only been here a couple of days, and already, people were coming out of the woodwork, offering to help.

Granted, she suspected that a lot of the people just wanted to get a peek at the boys, because who didn't love babies? But from the warm hugs and whispered condolences, she also knew that they sincerely cared about the fact that she had recently lost her husband. And if anyone thought that so soon after her husband's death, she shouldn't be marrying another man, no one said so. The only people who expressed outright disapproval were Cash's parents, but they obviously had their reasons. Other than their initial concern over such a hasty decision, Josie and Abigail had been nothing but supportive. Though Laura and Wyatt had agreed on a small quiet ceremony at the courthouse, her family had talked her into having a small ceremony at the main house, performed by the pastor.

It still wasn't going to be a fancy affair, just family, but having their pastor perform the ceremony somehow made her feel better. It hadn't occurred to her that she needed God's blessing on this marriage, but it felt like this was the missing piece. Even though they'd come to this decision in a split second, every prayer she'd uttered since then made her feel more and more like they were doing the right thing.

Barbara came out of the bedroom, cradling Garrett close to her. "Little Cody is still fast asleep, but this guy just seems to want all the excitement."

Sure enough, Garrett was in Barbara's arms, and he was looking around the room like he was taking it all in.

Laura smiled at her mother-in-law. "It's funny how even so young, the twins have their own personalities. Cody is much more mellow and can sleep through anything, but Garrett is constantly on the go."

"His father, God bless him, was the same way." Barbara chuckled as she smoothed the baby's hair. "He never was much of a sleeper. He just always wanted to be out, doing and seeing everything. He never wanted to miss out on anything."

Times like this, Laura could see the genuine love Barbara had in her heart, and that while they might disagree on things like the best way to arrange a room for the boys, she spoke with the same deep mother love that Laura had for her sons. Getting along with Barbara was difficult, but if Laura could continue finding common ground, it was all the more love for the boys to be surrounded with.

Josie seemed to sense the opportunity to

find ways to get along as well, because she smiled at Barbara and said, "He sounds like he must've been quite the handful."

Barbara nodded, adjusting Garrett in her arms. "And to think poor Laura has two of them. I just don't know how she's going to do it all on her own."

So much for that one shining moment where she could see Barbara as a grieving mother whose grandchildren were the only link to a son she'd dearly loved.

"Well, it's a good thing she's not doing it alone," Josie said. "That's why she's come home. We're all here for her. It will be so good for the boys to grow up here, just like we did, and being surrounded by all these people who love them."

Barbara looked annoyed for a moment, then she said, "We would have been there for them."

Feeling the strength of her family and Wyatt, Laura smiled. "And you still can be. As I have told you time and again, I want you to be part of the boys' lives. You're welcome to visit any time. And, as you've seen, we do have hookups for your motor home, so it wouldn't be any trouble."

Rather than looking pleased at Laura's

offer, Barbara only seemed more distraught. "But I'm going to miss so many of their milestones. Garrett rolled over yesterday, and we were not there to see it."

It felt unkind to remind her that even if they were back in Texas, they probably would've missed it as well, with the distance between them. No one could be there for every single moment, and Laura herself had barely caught it coming into the room with a load of boxes.

"We'll do our best to make sure you're there for as much as possible," Laura reassured her. "You're the only grandparents the boys have, and it's important for us to have you in their lives."

She'd already told Barbara this multiple times, and hopefully someday, Barbara would understand. None of this was meant as a slight against the older woman, and Laura prayed that they would someday be able to figure out a way for everyone to feel comfortable with the way things were.

Wyatt hated seeing the exhaustion on Laura's face. More so, he hated the strained expression as she tried placating Cash's mom. Barbara had always been a difficult woman, and they'd always done their best to honor her as Cash's mother. Cash used to say that it was easier to go along with what his mother wanted than to argue with her.

Even as adults, they'd typically taken the path of appeasing the woman who had a "my way or the highway" attitude toward her son.

But for the first time, as he saw the grieving woman holding her grandson, he realized the depth of Barbara's love. He saw the pain in her eyes as she looked from Laura down to the baby in her arms, and he could sense her fear. Barbara had just lost a son, and she was terrified she'd lose her grandsons as well.

Maybe she was difficult, but he also could see the reason behind it. She'd always wanted the best for Cash, so it made sense that she'd want the same for his sons. So how could he show her that even though Cash wasn't here to raise his boys, they would still be raised well? Wyatt watched as Barbara leaned down to nuzzle the baby, and Garrett giggled in response. That sound never failed to melt his heart, and Wyatt had to admit that in the short time he'd been more fully part of their lives, he'd grown to love them as his own.

Those nights on the road, lying in their hotel beds, when Cash had told him to love his family like his own, Wyatt hadn't known how it was possible. But now, he understood. It was the easiest, most natural thing in the world. While he still wished he could take back that day when Cash died, Wyatt was also grateful that he'd been given the opportunity to do right by Cash's family.

Including managing Cash's mother, who was blowing raspberries at the baby, and when Wyatt glanced at Laura, he saw that some of the tension had melted from her face.

Laura could have said no to Wyatt helping her. As he looked around the room at all the loving support she had from her own family, she probably would be fine without him. Sure, she might not have the health insurance she'd be getting upon their marriage tomorrow, but he had no doubt that the people surrounding them would never let them go without. Even the simple gesture of the casserole Laura had mentioned to him. He'd forgotten what the church family here was like. Sure, he went to church in Texas, but with being on the road so much, he'd never grown roots there. They'd barely arrived in Shepherd's Creek, and already they were being embraced like family.

Brady's phone rang, and after a short conversation, he turned to Wyatt. "That foal we were expecting was just born. You want to come with me to check it out?"

Wyatt had not had a chance to inspect the mare, or learn about much of his job duties, for that matter. But this seemed very much like what would eventually be his responsibility.

"Absolutely," Wyatt said.

As everyone exclaimed happily, he saw the smile on Laura's face.

"You want to come with us?" he asked.

She shook her head and gestured at Barbara and the baby. "No. I need to stay here with the boys."

"You should go," Barbara said. "I can take care of the babies for you for a while. Opportunities to see a newborn foal don't come very often."

Laura hesitated for a moment, and Wyatt knew she was torn. If anything, she needed a break from Barbara. As much as Barbara questioned Laura's abilities as a mother, Wyatt knew that Laura hated leaving the boys, even for a few minutes. However, this short time of letting Barbara watch the boys was a good opportunity for the women to learn to trust each other.

"It'll be fine," he said. "We're just going out to the barn. If we're needed, they can call us. We're five minutes away."

His reassurance seemed to be what Laura needed, because she nodded and stood. "It's been a long time since I've seen a newborn foal. I've always loved babies, whether human or animal."

The delight on her face warmed his heart, and it made him even happier that she'd agreed.

As they walked toward the barn, Wyatt could sense a lightness in Laura. Yes, she'd needed this break. Maybe tonight, after Barbara went back to her RV, and the boys were tucked in bed, they could sit on the couch with a cup of tea and talk about his recent revelations about Barbara. That was something he hadn't expected to develop in their relationship.

Every evening, after the boys were put to bed, Laura would make them both cup of herbal tea, and they'd just sit and talk. Until they'd begun that habit, he hadn't realized how much he needed something like that in his life. They'd always been friends, but this was starting to feel deeper, and the newfound connection was something Wyatt cherished.

They followed Brady to the mare's stall, and they were greeted by the sight of the cutest little black foal he'd ever seen. She had a few white specks in her coat, which Laura was the first to point out.

"Look at all those flecks. It's almost like stardust."

Brady laughed. "I think you're right. That's what I think I'll name this little filly. Stardust."

Brady's teenage daughter, Kayla, came bounding into the stables. "I did not just hear you name the horse without asking me," she said.

"Laura picked it out," Brady said. "Don't you think it fits?"

For a moment, Kayla looked a bit put out. But then she sighed. "It is the perfect name. But I get to name the next one."

"Deal," Brady said, ruffling his daughter's hair. While she pretended to not like it, and moved away, Wyatt saw the love in her eyes for her father.

They had recently learned that Kayla was not Brady's biological daughter, and regardless of biology, it was clear that a father and daughter could not have loved each other more had they shared blood.

Despite only having accepted the boys as his own a short time ago, Wyatt understood that feeling. Garrett and Cody were his, and he would do whatever it took to protect them.

He stole a glance at Laura, who was completely focused on watching the baby wobble on unstable legs. Some of the fatigue he'd seen in her earlier had faded from her face. Her hair was falling out of its ponytail, and a smudge of dirt streaked her cheek. Though he tried not to notice such things about his soon-to-be wife, Laura had never looked more beautiful to him.

He'd promised her a marriage in name only, and he intended to keep that promise. But moments like these, he wished they could have something more. Impossible, since it was Wyatt's fault that Laura was single in the first place.

Was it right to love the woman whose husband you had effectively killed?

Maybe he couldn't help the feelings that cropped up now and again. But he didn't have to act on them. These stolen moments where he thought he might feel something other than friendship for Laura, those were his and his alone.

Perhaps that was the price he had to pay for his role in Cash's death.

Wyatt would have the family, a wife beyond compare, and two boys whom he would always hold close in his heart.

But he would never have her love.

Chapter Five

Laura had never imagined that her wedding day could put so many turbulent emotions in her heart. She hadn't wanted a big fuss, since her first wedding had been practically her dream ceremony, other than the fact that Josie hadn't been there. Back then, she'd been angry with her cousin for not being willing to stand up with her, but Laura hadn't understood just how painful it had been for her to come home and face her estranged father as well as the ex-boyfriend who had broken her heart.

Thankfully, Josie and Laura had worked through those issues, and were now closer than ever. For this wedding, Josie was her maid of honor. Better still, Josie's ex-boyfriend, Brady, was now Josie's fiancé, and once again standing up as the best man. Funny how things came full circle in unexpected ways.

Even though Laura's uncle Big Joe had passed away, it felt like they were all a family again, better and stronger than ever.

Having them here, supporting her on this next stage of her life, gave Laura hope that everything was going to be okay.

Despite Laura's insistence on not making a big fuss, Josie and Abigail had decorated the archway in the backyard of the main house with flowers, and Laura and Wyatt stood under it, each one of them holding a twin, and Abigail and Kayla sitting on lawn chairs next to Cash's parents. She hadn't wanted to invite Cash's parents, but considering their RV was parked on the stable grounds, it would have been rude not to.

"Dearly beloved," the pastor intoned, "we are gathered here today to bless the union of this family in the sight of God."

As the prayer continued, she could feel Cash's parents' eyes on her, judging her. Not even the pastor's prayer to bless their marriage eased the butterflies in her stomach. Usually, prayer was the balm to everything that ailed her. Despite her earlier feeling that everything would be okay and that God was there for them, Barbara's icy glare made her question her decision.

This marriage was for the benefit of her sons. At this point in her life, that was all that mattered to Laura. She'd already had love and all the wonderful things a person intended to have in a marriage. She just hadn't known until it was too late that many of those things were a lie.

Better to marry based on friendship and the common goal of caring for her boys.

"I, Wyatt Anthony Nelson, take you, Laura Faith Fisher, to be my lawfully wedded wife, to have and to hold…"

As she looked up at the man promising to love, honor and cherish her, she felt a tremendous amount of guilt at the thought that Wyatt would never get to have that experience for himself. She almost wanted to stop the ceremony and tell them she couldn't go through with it because Wyatt deserved better. He deserved the love of a good woman. Before Cash had died, she would have said that he was the second-best man she'd ever known, Cash being the first. Now that she knew Cash's secrets, it was tempting to say that Wyatt was now the best, especially since he'd jumped in to take care of her and the babies. But that felt slightly disloyal and wrong, and she had a feeling that if she told Wyatt this, he wouldn't like it, either.

All she could do was pray that they were doing the right thing for the boys, and that somehow, they'd find a way to create their own personal happiness.

So when it came time for her to say, "I do," she did, and she prayed that she wasn't ruining Wyatt's life by doing so.

The rest of the ceremony was a blur, and she was thankful for that, in the sense that it meant everything went smoothly. Even the boys were behaving.

But then came the part she'd been dreading.

The pastor intoned in his low voice, "You may now kiss the bride," and Laura's stomach sank. They had discussed this the night before, quietly and privately. They had both agreed that for the sake of appearances, there would have to be a kiss.

Wyatt had told her that it would be gentle, quick and discreet. But as he leaned in toward her, waves of panic filled her. Cash had been the only man to ever kiss her. Even though she was filled with anger at him over what he'd done, her heart ached at the idea of this being just one more symbol of how all her hopes and dreams for the future had been shattered.

When Wyatt's lips brushed hers, it was a fleeting, gentle, tender touch, almost like butterfly wings. In that moment, all of her nervousness was forgotten. Something inside her changed, and she felt completely safe. Like this had been the right decision, and everything was going to be okay.

Just as quickly as the moment had come and passed, Wyatt took a step back, and when she looked into his eyes, she couldn't read the expression, except to say that it was as bewildering as all the jumbled up feelings inside her.

And that was it. They were married.

Josie immediately hugged Laura. "I pray you will have a long, happy, loving marriage."

It felt odd, accepting her cousin's congratulations when she wasn't marrying for love. But they probably could use all the prayers they could get. Their personal happiness had never factored into the equation. Would everything else they'd used as reasons for their marriage be enough?

Then Abigail came over and hugged her as well. "It was a beautiful ceremony. I hope God richly blesses you both with a life full of love."

The support from her cousin and sister made Laura feel even worse. She hadn't told them this was a marriage of convenience, and had been afraid to do so. Josie was finally getting her opportunity to have love at long last, and poor Abigail was still waiting to find the right man. It felt wrong to tell them that she had given up on love when they both were so hopeful.

"Thank you," Laura told them. "It means a lot to have your support."

"That's what family is for," Abigail said as she reached for Garrett. "And this little cutie was such a good boy for the wedding."

Her sister snuggled the baby next to her and covered him with kisses. Garrett squealed with delight, reminding Laura what a blessing family was.

She looked over at Wyatt, who'd just gotten a hug from Brady.

This might not have been the perfect wedding and marriage that so many dreamed of, but the love and support from their family made this far better than any story.

Laura turned her gaze to the Fishers, who looked like they'd rather be anywhere but here.

"I'm going to go talk to Mike and Barbara,"

Laura said, smiling at Abigail. "Do you mind keeping him a bit longer?"

"Mind?" Abigail adjusted the baby in her arms. "Never. I know you feel bad about accepting our help, but I'm so grateful to have these little guys here. It's like we have our family back together again."

Her sister kissed the top of Garrett's head. "I've given up on having a family of my own, so having them here is the next best thing."

Laura already had been feeling bad about her sister's unmarried state. But she hadn't considered how the idea of family would impact her as well.

"I'm glad we are able to make you feel better. But I hope you haven't given up on finding happiness for yourself. It's never too late."

Just because Laura had made a different choice for herself didn't mean Abigail couldn't find true love. Laura had never understood why Abigail had never met the right man. She'd always been the kindest, most selfless human being Laura had ever known. Josie's mother had died in childbirth, and Laura and Abigail's mother had died only a few years later, so Abigail had helped raise Laura and Josie. She'd been too young to take on that responsibility, and missed out on much of her own childhood to do so. But Abigail had never complained, nor had she ever spoken of regretting her actions.

"I'm forty-five years old," Abigail said. "Even if God put Mr. Right on my doorstep this very second, having a baby would be next to impossible. But also, if He hasn't seen fit to find me a husband at this point in my life, then I have to accept that maybe it's not His will that I'll ever marry. I'm at peace with that. I get a great deal of satisfaction working with the children here at the stables, and now you're here to give me my baby fix. What more do I need?"

Abigail gave the baby another kiss. "And this little guy needs his diaper changed. So I'm going to take care of that and you can handle Barbara."

Though Abigail's tone was light, Laura understood. As always, the topic of her sister's love life, or lack thereof, was off-limits.

Despite her sister's unwillingness to be candid about her romantic prospects, Laura found comfort in Abigail's words. Abigail lived a happy, full life without the benefit of marriage. While Laura technically had a husband, it lacked all the things most marriages had. In a sense, Laura and Abigail were the same, finding happiness in life without the benefit of a romantic partner.

Laura had already decided she didn't need romance in her life, but having her sister as an example of someone who could be perfectly happy without it made it seem even easier for her to do it.

She steeled herself to say hello to her in-laws, or former in-laws, or...what did she even call them now that her husband was dead, and she was married to another man? It was amazing how complicated things were, given the circumstances.

But she had to believe that God had brought them all together for a purpose, and having not grown up with grandparents, Laura would do whatever it took to make the relationship work.

Well, that didn't go as expected. Wyatt sipped his iced tea as he waited for Laura to finish putting the boys down for their nap. Her sister and cousin had set up a small nursery in the main house for the twins so Laura would have all she needed whenever she was there. Her family had thought of everything, and once again, Wyatt found himself thanking God for all the wonderful ways Laura and the children had been taken care of.

But as she came out of the house, laughing with her sister, both of them carrying plates of food for the wedding supper, the uneasy feeling he'd had since kissing Laura had returned. It seemed like the best idea, to have the traditional kiss at the end of the wedding, so that no one knew this was a marriage of convenience. But that small kiss they'd shared had completely upended Wyatt's world.

He wasn't supposed to have felt anything. He'd only given her the same gentle kiss he pressed to the boys' foreheads at night when he tucked them into bed. Laura wasn't one of the boys. She was a living, breathing, incredible woman who he thought he might have feelings for.

Falling for Laura would be the worst possible thing he could do in the situation.

But it was just one kiss.

Never to be repeated, and whatever longings it brought up in him, he would push them aside and ignore them.

Soon enough, he would forget. He would forget how it made him feel, and how, if they hadn't both been holding a baby, he'd have pulled her closer, deepened the kiss and given in to that small voice that occasionally asked him if maybe they could have a marriage for real.

They couldn't.

This marriage was Wyatt's penance for his sins. He didn't deserve the love of a woman like Laura. And he wasn't going to even try.

Brady sat down next to him. "It was a nice wedding," he said.

"I thought it went well," Wyatt agreed, trying to sound casual, like he hadn't just stabbed himself in the heart.

"Laura is a good woman," Brady observed, a look of concern on his face.

"I know," Wyatt said. "That's why I married her."

Odd conversation to have after a wedding, especially since they hadn't talked much about him marrying Laura, other than the strategic details.

For a moment, Brady remained silent, then he said, "I know why you're doing this."

Wyatt didn't say anything, but looked at the ground. Brady couldn't possibly realize all of Wyatt's reasons, but his friend knew him well enough that Wyatt wasn't sure he wanted to hear what he had to say. Still, he owed it to him to listen.

"I didn't try to talk you out of it, because I know both of you when your minds have been made up," Brady continued. "I know you have always felt responsible for Cash's well-being. Even as kids, we were always there, making sure he was safe, and cleaning up his messes. Just like that time you took the blame for denting his mother's car."

Wyatt chuckled at the memory. "If Barbara had known Cash did it, she wouldn't have let him go to rodeo camp with us. Cash still paid for the damage, so it wasn't like I lost anything, other than my reputation with Barbara, and she already hated me."

Though Brady laughed along with him, Wyatt could see the concern hadn't left the man's eyes.

"I know that's what you're doing now," Brady continued. "Like me, I'm sure you carry guilt over not having told Laura about his gambling addiction. And it's terrible, the way he left her and the boys with nothing. But it's not your responsibility to fix."

Brady didn't know the half of it. Yes, they both had guilt over not telling Laura about Cash's gambling problem. But Brady hadn't been responsible for Cash's death. Wyatt had.

Wyatt stared at his friend. "Why are you

telling me this now? Laura and I are already married."

Brady looked at him with compassion in his eyes. "In your marriage vows, you promised to love her. The promise you made to your wife and God isn't about fixing your guilt or making up for the way Cash wronged her, but about loving her."

Ouch.

He'd expected more opposition from Laura's family than he'd gotten, but he'd chalked up their support to wanting to be there for a widow and her children, as well as the fact that they'd all known each other forever. They knew he and Laura were friends and he'd take care of her, so they had nothing to worry about.

But this… Wyatt wasn't expecting this.

Of course he loved Laura. As a friend.

Brady placed a hand on Wyatt's knee. "I'm telling you this as a friend. As someone who almost married a woman to give a child a name because I thought it was the right thing to do. I will forever be grateful to Maddie for calling off our wedding, because Maddie knew that we didn't love each other, and we never would."

He gestured at his daughter, who was

laughing at something Josie, her soon-to-be stepmother, was saying. "Not getting married simply to give Kayla a father was the best thing for all of us."

"Why are you telling me this now?" Wyatt asked again. "Why didn't you try to stop the wedding?"

Brady looked at him solemnly. "I thought about it. I'd intended to have this talk with you last night at the stables, but you invited Laura. I saw how you looked at her. Maybe you're not ready to admit it to yourself or to anyone else, but you care for her."

How could he have been so transparent in those secret feelings that Brady had caught on so easily? He'd have to be more careful in the future. More than that, he'd have to spend more time talking to God about these feelings that kept popping up. He married Laura to honor God, not pursue his own agenda.

Wyatt took a deep breath. "Of course I care for her. That's why I married her."

"As a man cares for a woman," Brady said. "I think you two can love each other and have a full marriage. I remember the crush you had on her when we were kids. But she fell for Cash and you did the honorable thing and stepped aside because that's what you do.

You've always been the honorable one. But it hasn't escaped my attention every woman you've ever told me about that you've dated has resembled her in some way. Don't let your guilt get in the way of your heart. I think Laura is who you've been waiting for all along."

Wyatt stared at his friend. "I'm not going to profit from the death of my best friend."

Brady groaned. "I didn't mean it that way but, I guess that did sound a bit insensitive. I'm just saying that you could actually love her. I never even liked Maddie, which is why we would have never worked out. But you and Laura have always been close friends. You could have something really good with her, if you let yourself get past the guilt that drove you to marry her in the first place."

Wyatt supposed he shouldn't have been surprised that his oldest friend would have seen through this plan. But he didn't think Brady could spot so many flaws. Though, to be fair, Brady didn't know all of it. And Wyatt wasn't going to confess to Brady, or anyone else, what he had done.

Instead, he looked at Brady and said, "Laura and I are in agreement on what has to be. There are many different kinds of love.

I have familial love for her. She's not looking for romantic love, and neither am I. But thank you for your concern."

He was saved from Brady's response by Kayla running over to them, looking excited. "I did just what you said, Dad. I asked Laura if she would let me help babysit the twins sometimes, and she said yes."

Brady grinned at his daughter. "That's great. I'm sure it's just as much of a blessing to Laura as it is to you."

Wyatt nodded. "Absolutely. It was hard, packing up the house and trying to take care of the boys, so to have you around as a helper while she's unpacking would be great. Especially since I have the rodeo coming up this weekend. I don't want to leave them, but Laura made me promise."

"She was right to do so," Brady said. "We can't stop living simply because Cash died. He wanted that championship for you just as much as he wanted it for himself. When he talked about his successes, it was never just about him. But about the two of you. He believed in you, and you can't throw away your dreams because you feel guilty that he died."

Kayla groaned. "Gross. At least now I know that Dad gives his motivational speeches to his friends and not just me. I'm going to see how long until dinner. I'm hungry."

As she ran off, Wyatt couldn't help laughing. "She's a real spitfire, isn't she?"

"That she is." Brady laughed. "I just wish she knew that all those motivational speeches I give her are because I truly care. She's such a good kid, with so much potential."

Then he looked back at Wyatt. "Just like you. Losing Cash was a blow to all of us. The best way you can honor him is to do all the things with your life that he isn't going to get to do."

Easy enough to say when you didn't realize that Wyatt was the reason Cash was dead. Would Brady have that same faith in him, knowing that? Sure, were circumstances different, Wyatt would be telling himself the same thing about Cash. He might believe in all the things Brady was encouraging him about. But there was blood on Wyatt's hands, and no matter how hard he prayed, it wasn't going to go away.

"I'll do my best," Wyatt said, hoping it was enough to get Brady to change the subject.

But he should have known better. "I know you're just trying to get me to leave this alone. For now, I will. Just think about what I said. Really think about it," Brady reiterated, getting up and starting toward his daughter. "You both deserve real happiness."

Real happiness. Wyatt didn't deserve happiness.

Everything Brady had pointed to in terms of happiness belonged to Cash. Sure, he'd had moments of happiness since Cash's death, like when the boys smiled or did something that made his heart melt. Even yesterday with Laura in the barn, Wyatt had felt happiness. And that was what he would have to settle for in life.

The kind of happiness people like Brady had might not be Wyatt's, but Wyatt could still find contentment in the small moments that he already appreciated, and joy in knowing he was serving the Lord's command of taking care of widows and orphans.

It would be enough for him. It had to be.

He looked over at where Laura was laughing at something that Josie and Abigail were saying. It warmed his heart to see the three women together again, especially after the estrangement that had separated them. Both Laura and Cash had been heartbroken when Josie's father had refused to support their marriage, and Josie hadn't come to the wedding because of her personal issues. It had felt right, having Josie and Brady stand up for them at this ceremony.

Of all the things Wyatt was most grateful for with this tragedy, it was the way the family had come back together. Though Brady hadn't been joking about the low salary, Wyatt had felt himself richly blessed to be in a position where he could be here at the stables, giving back so much of what he had gotten from the experience growing up here. During those years, he'd never seen much of his father, and his mother hadn't been much of the motherly type. The people here had become his family. In a lot of ways, this was a homecoming for him as well.

He glanced around the backyard, noticing that while Cash's father was sitting in a chair, sipping his iced tea, Barbara was nowhere to be found. He hadn't seen her since they'd put the boys down for their nap after the ceremony.

He'd known this marriage would be hard on Cash's family, and even though Wyatt didn't always see eye to eye with Barbara, he knew Cash would've wanted him to look out for his mom.

Since everyone else was occupied, Wyatt

went into the house to look for her. The house was mostly quiet, except as he walked toward the back bedroom where they'd set up the porta cribs for the boys, he could hear Cash's mom speaking softly. When he peered into the room, she was sitting in the rocking chair, a sleeping baby in each arm, singing.

His heart ached at the sight. The older woman was dealing with several blows at once. The loss of her son, but also her grandchildren moving farther away. Sure, they'd said that they'd be moving to Colorado to be closer to the boys, but he'd overheard Cash's father telling Brady that his company had closed its Colorado office, so if they were going to move here, he would have to find another job. He'd been hoping that Brady would give him some connections, but there was nothing in the area that paid the kind of money Cash's father was used to making. Barbara might want to be here to be close to her grandsons, but it likely wasn't going to happen anytime soon.

Every minute Barbara spent here with the boys was a gift.

Quietly, he stepped away from the door, giving the grandmother time with the little boys she loved so much.

As he walked back into the other room, he ran into Laura.

"Have you seen Barbara?" she asked.

Wyatt nodded, gesturing toward the back bedroom. "She's snuggling with the boys, and I didn't have the heart to disturb her. She really loves them, and I feel for how much pain she must be in."

Laura gave him a sweet smile that was almost heartbreaking to look at. Her warm loving heart was everything a man could hope for. Though Brady had encouraged him to work on having a real marriage with Laura, his regret, even though Laura said she didn't need that kind of love anymore, was that he was denying another man the privilege of loving her.

"I'm glad she's got some time with them. Times like this remind me that even though Barbara and I disagree on so many things, at the very heart of it all is her love for the boys. I hope this makes her feel more secure in knowing we're all in this together."

A woman who could see it that way deserved to be loved. Though Laura said she was done with romantic love, it was inevitable that someone would see what he saw in her heart. Were that to happen, Wyatt would gladly stand aside for Laura to have a chance at happiness.

Though that thought was supposed to encourage him in his generosity toward Laura, he felt a pang of jealousy at the thought of another man holding her heart.

Odd, since he'd never felt jealous of Cash. Wyatt's hopes and dreams had never been about Laura, other than being genuinely happy for her having the life she'd always dreamed of. Now that those dreams were gone, Wyatt simply wanted what was best for her. More and more, Brady's words echoed in Wyatt's head.

Did Wyatt love her?

Gah, it didn't matter. He had to stop thinking this way. No good would come of it.

Laura was looking at him funny. "Are you okay?"

"Yes," Wyatt said. "Sorry. Just a little hungry, I guess."

"Good. Because the food is ready."

The warm smile she gave him spoke of care and compassion. They didn't need love. They could make their marriage work without it.

He followed Laura outside and everyone was laughing and talking. When he saw

Mike, he said, "Barbara is in snuggling the babies. I wasn't sure if I should disturb her or not, so I'll leave that to your judgment."

Cash's dad patted him on the shoulder. "Thank you. Barbara has been a wreck, thinking that she might be losing the boys, too, so it means a lot to see how hard the two of you are working to make sure we get to be a part of their lives. I know she can be pushy sometimes, but Cash was all we had, all she had, and his loss has been very hard on her."

The grief in the older man's voice was another confirmation that as difficult as dealing with Barbara was sometimes, they were doing the right thing.

Wyatt glanced over at Laura, who smiled at him. She was his wife, and even though it was hard, the difficulties they faced would be easier, knowing they were doing it together. He turned his attention back to Cash's father. "You may have lost Cash, but just remember, you have each other. It's clear that you love your wife very much, and I hope that I can be just as good of a husband to Laura as that."

Mike nodded slowly. "It's been hard on Barbara, watching Laura move on so quickly, but I suppose just as much as Barbara has needed me, Laura has also needed help."

"We've always been good friends," Wyatt said. "I could never take Cash's place, not in Laura's life, or in the boys'. Which is why it's important to both of us that the two of you are always part of our family. Nothing can replace Cash, but I hope that together, we can all make sure his legacy lives on."

His words seemed to make Mike feel better, because the older man's face softened, and as Laura gestured to the table, telling them all to take a seat, Wyatt realized he needed those words as well.

All this talk of a real marriage and what it meant to love Laura, it all came back to that simple goal. Preserving Cash's legacy. Because of Wyatt, Cash had no future. But he could ensure that Cash lived on. That would be Wyatt's focus.

Chapter Six

Laura cradled Cody against her as she tried to comfort him. He had been cranky when Wyatt had left this morning, but Laura had brushed off his concern because she didn't want him to miss this rodeo. He had sacrificed enough for her and the boys, and she wasn't about to let that stand in the way of his career. Wyatt was a great bronc rider, and he deserved the chance to compete.

Privately, she'd always thought that he was actually better than Cash, but it seemed like when it really mattered, Cash got the better horse. She'd thought it interesting that right up until the finals, Wyatt was always ahead in scores. But something about that final round made him choke, and she didn't know why. In the past, she'd been too busy encouraging her husband and congratulating him on his wins to talk to Wyatt about it. Cash had noticed as well. A couple of times, he'd told Laura that it had been in the back of his mind to throw a round or two so that Wyatt would have a chance at winning, but Laura had told him that Wyatt wouldn't have wanted to win that way. She had done everything she could to help her husband's career, and now, she had a different husband to support.

Wyatt.

She'd had to practically shove him out the door this morning, because he could sense that something was wrong, but she wasn't willing to let him give up his dreams for her. Not when he'd already sacrificed so much.

Which was why Laura was alone in the waiting room of a new pediatrician's office with a screaming baby in her arms, and another one fussing in the stroller. Cody was usually the calm one, but he'd been howling all morning, and now he was running a temperature.

People were staring at her, and it was hard not to tell them that she was doing the best she could with two babies. One who was just always cranky, and another who was obviously sick.

What if something was really wrong with Cody? Maybe she shouldn't have made Wyatt go.

Fortunately, they called her back, and the pediatrician, a kindly woman named Dr. Strutt, reassured her. Cody was going to be fine. A quick examination revealed her son had an ear infection, which was common in babies his age. She also took a look at Garrett, who was perfectly healthy. Just his usual fussiness. And, as the doctor pointed out, probably a little stressed because his normally calm brother wasn't feeling well and crying more than usual.

As she left the doctor's office, Josie called her back. Laura had left messages with her cousin and sister, hoping one of them could help her. Cash's parents had told her the day before that they had a busy day, full of appointments, so Laura hadn't wanted to intrude on their schedule.

But the stress in her voice must have been obvious to Josie, because her cousin immediately offered to meet Laura at the house so Laura could leave the boys with her and go to the pharmacy for Cody's prescription without a couple of screaming babies.

When Laura arrived at the house, Josie was already there, Kayla in tow.

"I hope you don't mind," Josie said after assisting Laura as she got the boys out of the truck. "Kayla is with me today for a shadow day as part of a school project, and she offered to come and help."

Laura took Cody out of his car seat and bounced the fussy baby in her arms. "As long as it's okay that she's around a sick baby. The pediatrician said it's just an ear infection, but I would hate to get anyone sick."

Josie reached out and took the baby into her arms as Kayla worked at getting Garrett out of his car seat. "We will be fine. That's the whole point of you coming home. You needed help, and we're here to give it to you. I'm not afraid of any little baby germs."

She said it in a funny little singsong voice as she looked down at Cody, and his wailing stopped for a moment.

"We are going to have a good time, aren't we, sweetie?"

He snuggled up to Josie, and Laura felt her muscles relax. She'd been so worried about the baby that it hadn't occurred to her just how much stress she was holding in.

"Thank you again," she said. "I just don't want to be a bother to anyone."

Cody started to scream again. "It's no bother. The sooner you get to the pharmacy and get his medicine, the sooner he'll be feeling better and back to his old self. Now go. We've got this."

Laura glanced over at Kayla, who was now playing with Garrett. Garrett had calmed down, and seemed like he was having fun with the teenage girl.

Even though Laura hated leaving the boys, Josie was right. The sooner she got the prescription, the sooner Cody would be feeling better and would be able to rest.

It was strange, driving into town by herself. Laura didn't think she had been alone in the car since before Cash had died. It almost felt wrong to be without her babies.

As she went past the local drive-through coffee shack, Laura remembered how this had been one of their favorite stops even as teens. She loved that it was still here, despite everything else that had changed.

She felt a new sense of freedom and happiness as she pulled in. Cody was getting medicine to feel better, she was doing all this without needing to infringe on Wyatt's time and despite all the hardships she'd faced lately, she knew everything was going to be okay. It had been forever since she'd had her favorite coffee treat. Though she didn't want to be a financial burden on Wyatt, he had given her access to a bank account that he said was to take care of household expenses, and that he didn't want her to worry about nickeling and diming everything.

She hadn't wanted to admit that it was far more money than she'd had in her account with Cash. She'd still be thrifty, because that was who she was, but it felt good to be honoring Wyatt's request that she be comfortable treating herself now and then.

Still, it felt weird to spend the money.

That first sip of iced mocha was better than anything she had remembered. It had been so long since she'd had one of these, let alone from her favorite coffee place. A month ago she would have never allowed herself this luxury. But as the blend of sweetness and tartness hit her tongue, Laura felt more peace than she'd felt in a very long time. If hope had a taste, she would say it tasted like iced mocha.

When she got to the pharmacy, it was also strange being there without the boys. One more thing she hadn't done since they'd been born. When she got to the counter, the prescription wasn't ready, so she walked around the store, enjoying the feeling of just being able to browse. It had been a while since she'd been able to do something like this, and it felt absolutely decadent, to be shopping and sipping an iced mocha.

Probably silly, making such a big deal of all of this, but it was interesting to look at her life and how drastically it had changed over the past couple of months. She would have never imagined that she'd be back in the small town where she'd grown up, at the pharmacy she'd known her whole life, waiting on a prescription for her son. And even though she had never imagined her life without Cash, that knowledge felt a little less heavy than it had since he'd died.

She paused at the book aisle, looking at the various titles. Just a few short months ago, all she'd done was read. The last little bit of her pregnancy, she'd been on bed rest, and the ladies at church kept her well stocked with books. Yet here she was, just a few months later, a mother, a widow, and she had no idea when the next time she'd be able to pick up a book just for the fun of it. The boys kept her too busy, and that was okay.

Still, she couldn't resist picking up the latest thriller by one of her favorite authors and scanning the back cover.

"Laura," a familiar voice said.

Laura turned and recognized Sara Windsor, a woman she'd gone to school with.

"Sara, it's so great to see you."

Sara gave her a warm hug, and once again, Laura was grateful that she'd returned home.

"I'm so sorry to hear about Cash," Sara said. "That must have been devastating for you. But I'm so glad you were able to come home and be with family again."

Laura smiled at her friend. "Yes. It's such a blessing to be home. I wouldn't have been able to do it without Abigail, Josie and Wyatt."

At the way Sara's brow furrowed, Laura remembered she'd forgotten someone. "And Brady, too. I can't believe I forgot him. I'm so glad he and Josie found their way back to each other."

Sara nodded slowly. "I think we all are. That just goes to show that love can withstand anything. I was surprised Wyatt came home, though."

Laura set the book back in the rack. "He promised Cash that he would take care of me and the boys if anything ever happened to him."

That seemed like a simple enough answer, even though it still felt weird, marrying again so soon after her husband's death. But all the details and reasons why it had been necessary were too personal to share with anyone. Some of it was because of the betrayal she'd felt. But also, there was a shame. She still didn't understand how she couldn't have known, and she didn't want to face the questions of anyone else. How could she admit that the fairy tale everyone thought they had was so riddled with lies?

Sara looked thoughtful, then said, "Wyatt always was a good man. I know everyone thought that Cash was the exciting one and that you were so lucky to have him. Everyone wanted to be in your shoes, but I always thought Wyatt was the better of the two. He was just always so steady, someone you could count on. I hope you don't mind my saying so, but there are going to be quite a few people disappointed that he's been taken off the market."

Even though Laura and Wyatt had discussed the idea of romance and Wyatt's romantic prospects, and Wyatt had assured her that it wasn't something he needed in his life, Sara's words made her question it. Was she cheating him out of the opportunity to have real love?

But she wasn't going to dwell on that right now. Instead, she smiled at Sara, and said, "I hope I didn't ruin anything for you. You were always a good friend, and I'd hate to think that I snatched Wyatt out from under you."

Sara laughed. "Oh no. It's been Matt Carlson for me ever since second grade. But he ran off and joined the army, and his brother Rex said he is happily married to the military. He never took notice of me. Even though Wyatt is a great guy, no one can compare to Matt in my eyes."

For a moment, Laura felt sorry for the other woman, but Sara seemed to sense that.

"Now, don't go feeling sorry for me. I could have gone on a hundred dates, with different men, and I tried. But I just never experienced anything like I did with Matt, and I don't want to settle for anything less."

They called her order number over the loudspeaker, and Laura smiled at Sara again. "That's me. I need to run, but it was really great catching up. Let's get together sometime and have a more proper chat."

Sara gave her another quick hug. "I'd like that."

They exchanged cell phone numbers, and it felt good to know she was already reconnecting.

Even though Laura had put the book back, when she had the prescription, she couldn't help wandering over and grabbing it again. Sure, she was busy with the boys. But everyone had been telling her to relax more, so maybe, in the evenings, once the twins had gone to bed, this would be something she could do for herself.

All in all, when Laura returned home, she was feeling pretty good. What had started out as a bad day had boosted her spirit, because she could see the system of support around her, and it made her feel less alone. And, when Wyatt came home, he'd be reassured because he would see that even with a sick child, she'd managed quite nicely without him.

They hadn't talked about the possibility, but maybe, once Laura was on her feet, she could set Wyatt free so that he could find someone to love. She'd already experienced it, so it wasn't a need she had, but after talking to Sara, she had to wonder, how did Wyatt really feel about the lack of love in his life?

Wyatt had done a good thing for her, and it was only fair that if she had the chance to help him find some of the contentment he'd brought to her, that she'd do the same for him.

Not even the sight of Barbara's car in front of her house could ruin Laura's good mood. At least not until she opened the front door. Laura's stomach sank. Barbara was pacing the living room, holding a screaming Cody while Garrett wailed in his bouncy seat. Kayla sat in the chair in the corner, looking terrified.

"Where were you?" Barbara demanded.

Laura held up the bag from the pharmacy. "Getting the prescription for my son."

She set everything on the coffee table and took the medicine out of the bag. "If you give me just a moment to prepare the dose, I can give it to him, and the pediatrician said he'd be feeling better very soon."

Barbara continued to glare at her. "How could you leave him alone when he's sick?"

Not this. Laura went into the kitchen and prepared the dropper of Cody's medicine. Then she held her arms out for her son. "I'm not going to take a sick baby out."

Barbara stared at the medicine in Laura's

hand, not giving up her grip on the baby. "How do I know that's the right dose? Do you know how to properly give the baby medicine?"

She seriously was not doing this. Laura took a deep breath, and prayed for guidance before answering. "The pediatrician explained everything to me, and the pharmacist also went over it. I'm quite capable of getting my son his medicine. Now please, give me my son."

Then she gestured at Garrett. "Why don't you comfort Garrett instead?"

Barbara handed Cody to her, and Laura cradled her little boy. "It's okay, sweetie. We'll get this medicine in you, and you'll be feeling better in no time."

She kissed the top of the boy's head, and he stopped crying long enough for her to squirt the medicine into his mouth. He seemed to like it, and started sucking on the syringe.

"Good boy," she said. "You like that?"

He looked confused for a moment and his eyes filled with tears again.

Poor baby. His ears must really hurt.

She turned to Kayla. "Were you able to give him a bottle while I was away? Where's Josie anyway?"

Poor Kayla looked like she was about to

cry, and Laura realized that Barbara must've been pretty hard on her. Kayla picked up a bottle from the side table. "Mrs. Fisher said it wasn't his feeding time and she told me to take it away."

Laura held her hand out for the bottle. "I set his feeding times, not her."

She looked over at Barbara, who still stood there, arms crossed, staring at her. Despite the concern Barbara had exhibited for her boys, Garrett still remained in his seat, crying. He was probably hungry, too. Laura would take care of him as soon as she got his brother settled.

She took the bottle, then set the medicine syringe on the table as she adjusted Cody in her arms and started feeding him.

Cody chugged it down greedily. Though he definitely was in pain, his crying had more likely been because he was starving. He'd been screaming too hard earlier in the day to eat much, and the pain medicine the doctor had given him in the office must've finally kicked in enough for his hunger drive to override his pain drive. But Barbara hadn't noticed that.

It felt good to know that Laura understood her son far better than the older woman who was still glaring at her.

"Thank you, Kayla." Laura sat down next to the teenager. "Do you want to finish feeding him? I know you've been asking to spend more time with the boys, and it doesn't seem like you've gotten much of a chance."

Though Kayla still looked a little scared, she nodded. "My dad had an emergency in the barn, and he asked Josie if she would come help. She said she'd only be gone for about fifteen minutes, and she had faith in me that I could handle this." Then she looked downcast. "But I guess I can't."

Laura handed the teenager her baby. "Yes, you can. You asked me the other day if you could babysit sometimes, and I said yes because I trust you. Now I'm going to go make Garrett a bottle because he's probably hungry, too."

"You would leave my grandchildren with a child?" Barbara practically screeched as she confronted Laura.

Laura glanced at Barbara. "Absolutely I would. As we've moved in, Kayla has been here, helping me with the boys. She's kind, loving and very mature and responsible."

Before Barbara could answer, the front door opened, and Josie walked in. "Sorry about that," she said. "Brady's barn emergency took longer than expected."

Then, sensing the tension in the room, she said, "Is everything all right?"

Barbara took a step toward her. "I can't believe you left my grandchildren with a child."

Laura bit back a groan. Hadn't she just addressed this issue?

Josie squared her shoulders. "Kayla is nearly sixteen. She is growing into a fine young woman who wants to be a pediatrician. She loves children and is good with them. I would trust Kayla with any child. However, if you're looking for qualifications, Kayla passed the babysitter's course at the rec center I work for with flying colors, and she is certified in CPR. There's no one I would trust more than Kayla."

Laura glanced over at Kayla and smiled. Kayla had told her all of that when she'd asked if she could be put on a list of potential babysitters for the twins. But it did a funny thing in Laura's heart to see the depth of love and support Kayla and Josie shared.

Josie was going to make a great stepmother, and it gave Laura even more hope that the love Wyatt already had for her sons would continue to grow.

Only that didn't seem to impress Barbara. "But he's sick. You left your sick child." She gestured at the coffee table, where Laura had set the things she brought with her into the house. "What do you do? You go out gallivanting. Buying a fancy coffee drink and a trashy novel? What kind of mother are you?"

"A very good one," Josie said just as Garrett let out a wail.

Laura started for her other son, but Josie held up a hand. "Let me take care of him. I only got to cuddle Cody, and I want some Garrett time before I go back to help Brady with the rest of what he needs."

Josie paused before picking up Garrett. "But Barbara, you are completely wrong about Laura. She's the best mother I've ever seen, and I work with a lot of families. Those boys are everything to her. You need to start giving her more credit."

Laura's throat tightened at her cousin's words. Growing up, they had been thick as thieves, until teenage drama and Josie's disagreements with her father had put a wedge between them. Laura would have never imagined coming to this place in her adult life with Josie being her strongest supporter, but having her cousin here for her now meant the world to her.

"Credit?" Barbara gestured around the house. "Look at this mess. My grandchildren are living in filth."

For the first time, Laura noticed what a disaster the house was. It had been a hectic morning, and she'd intended to clean things up once everything settled down. Wyatt had forgotten the trash she'd set by the door for him to take out when he left, and when she was carrying the boys out to the car, she'd bumped it with the car seat, and it had gone flying, creating a mess. Laura grimaced as she saw that the front of the television was coated with coffee grounds. But it was more than that, because the kitchen was also in disarray since Laura hadn't had time yet to clean up from breakfast. But she also noticed that things looked even worse than when she'd left.

Josie must have seen where Laura was looking, and hastily said, "That's my fault. I intended to get it all cleaned up by the time you got back, except Brady called. I was shaking Cody's bottle to mix the formula, and the cap came off, sending formula flying everywhere. I'll help you put everything to rights."

She held up the bottle she'd been making for Garrett. "And now I know to secure the bottle better."

At least that was one explanation.

"The laundry everywhere is my fault," Kayla said. "Cody spit up all over his outfit, and I was trying to find him something else, but in my hurry to get to the door when Mrs. Fisher came, I tripped on it, and dragged it with me, but I promise, I'll clean everything up."

Laura took a deep breath as she looked at the worried expressions on Josie's and Kayla's faces. She wasn't mad at them. But she could see where Barbara was absolutely furious.

"It's okay. These things happen. I often use the time when the boys are sleeping to catch up on stuff like this, and it was just bad timing that Barbara arrived when she did."

Even though Laura felt like crying, she put a smile on her face and looked over at Barbara. "I'm sorry that you walked in on such a bad day, but as you can see, there is a reasonable explanation for everything. It's hard to stay on top of things with a sick baby, and everyone did the best they could. But we're a team, and we're going to get through this together."

Though the rage didn't leave Barbara's face, both Josie and Kayla looked relieved. However, the idea of being a team and being in it together was what had given Laura the most confidence in the situation. This was why she'd come home.

"And just how did Cody get sick?" Barbara demanded. "You promised me you were going to keep me informed of their health and their doctor visits, and how do I find out? Would you have even told me?"

Once again, Laura took a deep breath, said another little prayer before answering. "I hadn't had the chance yet. When Cody woke up this morning, he was burning up with fever, and my first thought was to get him medical attention. Which is what I did. I knew you had a busy day today, and I didn't want to bother you. I had planned on letting you know everything once things calmed down. Maybe you should have a little faith in me."

It had been wrong to hope that Barbara would have been won over by that argument. The all too familiar expression of fury on Barbara's face didn't change.

"Faith in you? You stole my son, you squandered his money, and now his baby is sick with a mysterious illness. Why would I have faith in someone like you? The only notable thing you've ever achieved in your life is becoming a rodeo queen. You can't even take care of yourself. My son is barely cold in his grave, and you married the first cowboy that came along so you wouldn't have to do anything with your life."

The insults hit Laura straight in the solar plexus. She'd heard much of this before, but not all at once. Barbara had never dared speak so openly against her in front of anyone but Wyatt before, so this felt even more demeaning. And she hadn't been accused of squandering Cash's money before. It would've been so easy to simply say no, Cash did it. He gambled it all away and left me with no choices. But somehow Barbara would make that her fault, too.

Instead, Laura pulled together the last bit of self-respect she had left, and said, "Garrett has an ear infection. It's very common in babies his age, and in a few days, he'll be as good as new. As for all of the other horrible things you've just said about me, I'm not going to keep defending myself to you. In fact, I'm going to have to ask you to leave until you can be more civil to me."

Her heart thudded heavily in her chest, but she was proud of herself for being able to speak clearly and firmly.

She didn't know where that last sentence had come from. It wasn't like her to dismiss Barbara. In fact, she couldn't remember a time when she'd ever done so. But somehow, being back with her family, having Wyatt stick up for her the times he had, and even Josie, just now, made her realize she didn't have to take it.

Cash had kept secrets and pretended things were fine when they weren't because he'd been so terrified to rock the boat with his mother, and because of that, he'd left his family destitute. Her boys deserved a better example. And thanks to being in a loving environment, Laura was learning how to be that example.

She could love Barbara, but she didn't have to let Barbara walk all over her.

Barbara sputtered, like she didn't have the words to respond. Josie stepped out of the kitchen, still feeding Garrett.

"The door," Josie said. "I think it's time you leave. It's been a stressful day for Laura, taking care of the sick baby, and you're not helping."

Barbara glared at Laura again. "Fine. But don't think that you can keep my grandchildren away from me."

"I would never dream of doing so," Laura said. "But in my home, you need to have a little more respect for how I do things. They might be your grandsons, but I am their mother, and I know what's best for them."

It wasn't until Barbara left that Laura felt herself relax. Tears began to flow down her face. "Thank you," Laura said. "I don't know what I would have done without you."

Josie adjusted the baby in her arms and came over and put an arm around Laura. "She's acting completely inappropriately toward you, and I'm glad you stood your ground."

Then Josie turned to Kayla. "I know you've always been taught to respect your elders, but you should also know that the way Barbara spoke to you is not okay. I'm sorry you got brought into the middle of this."

Laura went and sat next to Kayla. "I agree." She gave Kayla a little squeeze, then said, "I meant what I said. I trust you with the boys, so don't take any of her words personally. Thank you for being here with them, and thank you for putting up with her nonsense."

Kayla nodded and squeezed Cody tighter to her. "Thank you for trusting me with them. I really do love them, and I hope I can spend time with them again soon."

Smiling warmly at the girl, Laura said, "I will definitely keep you in mind the next time I need someone to watch them."

Josie held Garrett, who had almost finished his bottle and was dozing off, out to Laura. "Now that I've had my cuddle time, I need to get back to the barn. But if Barbara shows back up, feel free to give me a call. I'll bring Brady with me, too. And as soon as I'm done there, I promise I'll be back to clean up this mess. You shouldn't have to deal with it alone."

She handed Laura the baby and his bottle, then looked over at Kayla. "I was supposed to bring you back with me, but as long as Laura doesn't mind having you hanging out for little while longer, I don't mind if you do."

Both the medicine and the bottle seemed to be taking effect on Cody, who was nearly asleep in Kayla's arms.

"Let's get the boys put to bed," Laura said. "Then you can go help your dad and Josie. A bit of a compromise."

Josie smiled, and as she headed for the

door, she paused. “Oh, and that book you just got? When you’re done with it, can I borrow it? It might not be to Barbara’s taste, but I have been dying to read that one.”

Her cousin’s words gave Laura confirmation that she wasn’t a bad mom for wanting a book to read during her down time. It gave her a little more confidence that she really did know what she was doing. Barbara tried to take that from her, but she wasn’t going to succeed. As she shifted the boy into her arms to get him ready for his nap, a feeling of deep contentment filled her. Yes, it had been a hard day, but she was figuring it out.

Driving home Sunday night, Wyatt still couldn’t believe he’d won. His first rodeo back, and he’d done it. It almost felt wrong, winning after Cash’s death. But he’d promised Laura and Brady, and even though he didn’t much like the idea of celebrating, it seemed right to be doing it for them. It wasn’t that he’d ever considered quitting, but he had to be honest, he didn’t have the same drive to win that he once had. Some might call him foolish, considering this was the thing he’d worked for his whole life. Being in the rodeo was all he had ever wanted to do, but there was no sweetness in his victory.

What people didn't realize about his friendship with Cash was that in some ways, Cash was the rodeo to him. Every memory he had of being in the rodeo was all about his relationship with Cash. As much as he loved the thrill of the win, it felt empty without Cash by his side to celebrate. It felt worse, wondering if the reason he won was because Cash wasn't there. True, Cash and Wyatt had always jockeyed for first, but how could it be called a victory when his biggest competition was gone?

Pulling into the driveway in front of his new home, Wyatt felt like an imposter. All of this should have been Cash's. The wife, the children, the fat check in his pocket. As he pulled up to the house, the police cruiser parked in front made his heart jump up to this throat.

What happened?

He got out of his truck as fast as he could and ran up the steps to the house as he prayed that everyone was okay.

Wyatt opened the door, and Laura was crying, talking to a sheriff's deputy.

"Wyatt," she said. "I'm glad you're home."

"What's going on here?" he asked.

The deputy turned to look at Wyatt. "I'm here for a wellness check as well as to follow up on a complaint of abuse and neglect. I was led to believe there are two babies here in imminent danger."

Wyatt stared at the deputy, then at Laura, before turning his attention back to the officer. "There must be some mistake. Laura is an amazing mom, and the boys are well taken care of."

The deputy remained expressionless. "I'm just here to check on the babies. We were told the boys were left home alone without adequate supervision and that they were living in filth, which contributed to one of them becoming ill." He looked down at his notes. "There was some concern that due to the child's illness, there was risk of immediate harm."

None of this sounded anything like Laura. Though Wyatt's heart still thundered in his chest at having his family under attack like this, he felt slightly better knowing that this all had to be a terrible misunderstanding. Still, he sent a quick prayer that this would all be sorted out soon.

"This is definitely a mistake," Wyatt said.

"I'm just trying to get to the bottom of this," the deputy responded.

The front door opened, and Brady, Josie and Abigail entered.

"What's going on here, Dave?" Abigail asked.

The deputy explained everything he had just told Wyatt, and it still didn't make any sense. Who would think that Laura was a bad mom? Despite Wyatt's prayers, he still had a sick feeling in his stomach.

"There has to be a misunderstanding," Brady said. "Laura has been here with the boys and hasn't left for days. Little Cody has an ear infection, so they've stayed home. I can personally attest to that."

The deputy checked his notes then said, "What about Friday afternoon? Can you verify her whereabouts then?"

Josie looked over at Laura, then said, "Could he be referring to when you went to the drugstore to pick up Cody's medicine?"

"It's the only time I've left the house," Laura said.

Then she squared her shoulders and looked at the deputy like she meant business. "I know what this is about. I know you can't say who made the complaint, but I'm guessing it was my former in-laws, and they were concerned about the boys. I did go to the pharmacy Friday afternoon, and I left my sons in the care of my cousin. Josie got called away on an emergency, and she left Kayla to take care of them. However, at fifteen, and having taken a babysitting course as well as being certified in CPR, Kayla is well-qualified to watch the boys for an hour or so while I ran errands. My former in-laws took offense to this decision, and now it seems they're making a big deal of it."

Laura pulled her cell phone out of her pocket. "I have thirty missed calls and multiple text messages from Barbara Fisher this evening that I haven't returned because I've been extremely busy caring for my sons. I imagine that's what prompted the call for you to come check on them. I'm sorry you wasted your time on a trip out here. But everything is on the up-and-up, and once again, I'm sorry you've wasted your time."

The look on Laura's face made Wyatt's heart sink. She'd told him about Cody getting sick and having a confrontation with Barbara, but he'd thought everything seemed to be resolved. How could Barbara stoop so low? And yet, watching the strength coming from Laura, Wyatt could honestly say he'd never been more proud of her.

"I can verify that," Josie said. "And, I can further corroborate what Brady said about Laura having not left. I'm happy to testify to Laura's good parenting skills. There's a reasonable explanation for every accusation that's been made."

"I'm also happy to give testimony," Abigail said. "Come on, Dave. You know us. Working with the kids at the stables, we know what abuse looks like. Laura is one of the best mothers I've ever known."

The deputy nodded slowly. "I'm not doubting you," he said. "Kayla has babysat for my kids, so I know she's trustworthy. But we have to take every accusation seriously and investigate, regardless of our personal feelings and how well we know the people involved."

He turned his attention back to Laura. "So if you wouldn't mind taking me to see the boys, I would appreciate it."

Laura looked dejected. "I just got them to sleep," she said. "But I don't have anything to hide, so I don't mind."

Wyatt felt helpless as he watched Laura lead the officer into the boys' room. He was in agreement with Laura about having nothing to hide, and with the simple explanation he'd heard, he knew there was nothing to worry about. But this invasion of privacy felt violating.

He couldn't believe that Cash's parents would put them in this situation. How could they be so selfish?

Sure, Kayla was technically just a teenager, but she was one of the most responsible kids he'd ever known. She'd been a big help to them when they were moving in, and the boys loved her already. It did feel good to know that the deputy himself used Kayla as a babysitter. But how was he supposed to handle this constant attack?

Brady patted him on the back. "It's going to be okay. Josie told me about what happened, and it's clear that this is just Barbara's meddling. Nothing will come of it—you'll see."

Though clearly the deputy was familiar with the family, and Brady sounded cheerful about the situation, Wyatt hated the fact that an accusation had even been made. Yes, Barbara made snide comments. But to actually call the authorities? That was going too far. His family was under attack, and he felt powerless to stop it.

Checking on the boys meant waking them up, and it pained Wyatt to see the confused little faces as the deputy picked up the boys and examined them. None of them deserved this, especially not the children.

Once the officer looked over the twins and ascertained that everything was okay with them, he left, saying that since he didn't believe the boys were in any immediate danger, he'd have one of the child services officers investigate further.

"It's going to be okay," Josie said, putting her arm around Laura, who held her babies tight against her.

Wyatt wanted to hold them as well, but Laura was their mother, and she needed the comfort of having them in her arms.

Abigail came to the other side of her sister and did the same. Now, more than ever, Wyatt was grateful Laura had her family to support her. But she shouldn't have had to go through this to begin with.

By the time they got everyone out of the house, and the boys back to sleep in Laura's arms, Wyatt was exhausted. And from the look on Laura's face, she was even more so.

"Let's put the boys to bed so we can sit and relax," he said.

Laura shook her head. "I can't. I know that police officer was just doing his job, but I can't stop thinking of his hands on my babies. I just need to hold them."

She still cradled them close to her. He gestured to her favorite spot on the couch. "Go, sit, and I'll make you some herbal tea. You've had a rough night—you deserve to relax."

When he returned to the living room, Laura was snuggling the boys, tears running down her face.

As he set the tea on the coffee table, he said, "None of this is your fault."

Wyatt sat next to her, put his arm around her and pulled her close. "You are the best mom, and anyone who can't see that is clearly blind. We'll get through this together."

Cody stirred in her arms. "I hate to be selfish, but can I have him for a bit? I need some cuddles."

The expression on Laura's face softened. "Of course. I'm so sorry. You've probably been just as worried as I have, and I've been hogging them all night."

Laura adjusted her hold on the boys and handed Cody to him.

Cody's eyes blinked open and stared up at him.

"Hey, little buddy." Wyatt smiled at the little boy and was rewarded with a sleepy grin that told him that no matter what, everything was going to be okay. What they were going through, it would eventually be worth it. They'd figure things out.

After he smoothed the boy's hair, Cody's eyes fluttered closed again and the baby snuggled up to him.

Such love and trust, and Wyatt felt like he was letting the baby down. He'd gone on one trip and his family was being threatened.

Laura leaned her head against his shoulder and looked up at him. "If I'm such a good mom, why can't Cash's parents see that? I'm trying to be loving and patient, knowing that they've lost a beloved son. I lost my husband, and my sons are without their father. How does she think that making things worse for us would make her feel better?"

Wyatt gave her a gentle squeeze. "For her, it's not about you. It's about her feelings of helplessness, her pain at losing her son. Despite her cruel words to you, I don't think that she has thought much about your feelings at all."

Though he had meant for his words to be comfort to her, they also comforted him. He had to remember that none of this was personal, as much as it felt like it was. But watching the deputy inspect his children like they were objects, it broke something in him loose. They might not technically be his sons, at least biologically, but the day he'd married their mother, they had become his in his heart. This was Wyatt's family, and he wasn't going to stand idly by as they were being threatened.

"I'm going to take a break from the rodeo circuit for a while," he told Laura. "I know you support my career, and that means the world to me. But the boys are more important to me than any championship, and I'm not going to stand for the Fishers making trouble every time I'm out of town. I have enough in the bank that we don't have to worry about money. But I'm not going to leave you to face them alone ever again. Even though we talked to a lawyer in Texas, I'm going to talk to one here, just to make sure all of our bases are covered."

Instead of looking pleased, Laura only seemed upset at his words. "I told you I don't want us to be a burden on you or interfere with your career. I can't let you make this sacrifice."

He stared at her for a moment, then said, "And I can't risk whatever mess they're going to make of our lives, especially as that affects our children. Coming home to having the police here, invading our lives, I'm sorry. I can't allow that to happen again."

The look of anguish on Laura's face only grew worse. "How is that fair for you to give up on your life? Your dreams? Yes, Cash was your friend, and you promised him to look out for us, but this is above and beyond."

She'd hate him if she ever discovered the truth. Instead, he said, "I understand what you're saying, but the thing you didn't count on was that when you marry someone, you pledge your life to them. It isn't about what I want, or my dreams, but what's best for our family. I knew that going into our marriage, and I made that choice willingly."

Laura had never been the kind of person to give up easily, so he wasn't expecting her to meekly agree. But she did surprise him with the way she smiled, then said, "Okay. I know you're not going to give in on this point, but I do think we need to find common ground. I'm not willing to let you give up your rodeo career. You've only got a couple of good years left, and I want to see you make your dreams come true. So what's the compromise?"

Compromise.

That almost seemed like they were in a real marriage. Something about that made Wyatt warm inside. He thought again to Brady's words, feeling the warmth of the woman next to him. True, he'd only put his arm around her in comfort, but it was easy in this moment to wonder if perhaps they could have something more.

Wyatt shook his head and pulled away from Laura slightly. No. That wasn't what he was here for. Nor was it what they'd agreed to. It was wrong of him to even consider the thought of having a real marriage with her. What he needed, what Laura needed, was the safety and stability of the family without the drama and the pressure of a romantic relationship.

So where did that leave them? He thought about Laura's idea of compromise. "Do you have any ideas?"

Laura looked down at the baby in her arms, then back at him. "We could travel with you."

"The rodeo is no place for babies. How would we take care of them on the road?"

Laura shrugged. "Lots of people bring their children to rodeos. We could make it work."

Was he a fool for considering it? But it was a compromise. And while he wasn't thrilled with the idea of having the boys on the road with him, it also wasn't the worst idea in the world. Before the babies came, Laura had gone with them to several rodeos. Lots of the families went to the rodeos, and many of them were friends. It wasn't ideal for raising babies, but they could manage.

Wyatt smoothed Cody's hair, hoping that he was making the right decision for the baby. "I suppose it wouldn't do any harm to give it a try," he said. "We'll see what happens with the police investigation, and as long as there's no problem there, with us taking the boys, we'll test it out for my next rodeo."

Chapter Seven

Being on the road again with Wyatt seemed almost like old times. Almost. Back in the day, it had been her, Cash and Wyatt. One of them would sleep in the back seat while the other two hung out up front, one driving and the other riding shotgun to keep the driver awake.

Now, Wyatt was driving, Laura had shotgun and the two boys were in the back in their car seats. They were headed to Utah, which meant long hours on the road for their first trip. It was strange, not having Cash teasing her about her choice of music. In fact, when she changed it to her favorite praise-and-worship station, Wyatt turned up the volume.

She glanced over at him. "I didn't know you liked this kind of music."

He laughed. "Cash hated it. I like his music, too, so I never argued with him about the radio station, but I always loved it when you put on your music. I just wasn't going to get in the middle of a fight between you and Cash."

Laura laughed along with him. Though he'd called it a fight, it was more just them ribbing each other. Some days, she still thought she'd like to hear Cash teasing her about her music. But then she remembered what he'd done to her, and even though she was working on forgiving him, she also knew she couldn't go back. Her memories of Cash weren't terrible, and she could look back on them with fondness. But had he survived, and come back to her with all the knowledge of what he'd done, she wasn't sure how she would have been able to look at him the same again.

The fairy tale wasn't what everyone made it out to be.

She started singing along when her favorite song came on, and even the boys sounded like they were making happy noises in the back. Cody's ear infection had cleared up, and he was doing much better. The child services investigation had been closed just as quickly as it opened, and they'd found no fault with Laura as a parent. The lawyer had also reassured them and given them tools for future interactions with Barbara. It was like everything was back to normal again. Praising God with song seemed like the perfect thing to do.

"It sounds real pretty when you sing," Wyatt said. "I don't think I've heard you sing before."

Laura stopped, then laughed, a little self-conscious. "I usually don't sing in front of anyone. I'm not sure what came over me."

"Don't stop on my account," he said. "It sounded nice."

The funny thing about Wyatt was that she'd loved the way he encouraged her. He'd always been a good friend, and if she had to pick anyone to take this journey with her in this rocky section of her life, it would be him.

He glanced over her, a boyish grin on his face. "What's got you smiling like that?"

"You," she said, realizing after she said it, she sounded kind of flirty.

For a moment, he looked a little surprised, but just as quickly, he appeared to recover. "What do you mean?"

At least he was giving her the chance to

elaborate and make up for her gaffe. "I know you don't like it when I express gratitude for everything you've done for me, but I was just thinking that, of all the people in the world, you're the one I trust the most to walk this stage of life with me. We've been friends a long time, and it means the world to me to have your friendship."

She emphasized the word *friendship*, hoping that it made up for accidentally sounding flirty. Right now, they had a good thing going, and she didn't want to ruin it.

Wyatt looked embarrassed, but then said, "You've been a good friend to me as well. I would never let you do this alone."

Another song Laura liked came on the radio, so rather than continuing the conversation, she turned up the volume.

They'd gone on dozens of road trips together, but this one felt different. Not just because they were man and wife, and her twin babies were cooing in the backseat, but there was a new energy between them. As she stole a glance at him focused on the road, for the first time, she saw Wyatt as a man. Yes, she knew he was male, but this vision of him as a man made her aware in a new way.

He'd always been nice to look at, at least that's what people said, but this was the first time she saw for herself. Really saw. She loved the light in his eyes, the crinkles at their sides and that funny little crooked tooth you saw when he smiled.

Wyatt used to joke that he knew all the buckle bunnies at rodeos wanted from him was his paycheck, because no one could love a beat-up cowboy who walked with a slight limp when he was tired, and was covered in scars from all of his mishaps, including one on the side of his face. That was a reminder to him of his failed attempt at bull riding. He'd been fortunate that it hadn't been worse, and he used to joke that every time he looked in the mirror, he remembered that he preferred bronc riding because it was safer.

Laura chuckled to herself. As if riding an untamed horse was at all safe.

Wyatt looked over at her. "Since when is a car insurance commercial funny?"

She smiled at him, noticing that he had a twinkle in his eyes. But it was hardly appropriate for her to admit that to him. Or to admit that she was thinking that despite all of his protestations, he was quite an attractive man.

Instead, she said, "I was just thinking how funny it is the way things turn out."

The reassuring smile he gave her warmed her heart and created a small stirring in her stomach.

Was she attracted to him?

The physical features she'd been admiring in him weren't what most people would consider as making a person handsome, but to her, they showed his strength of will, character and even his sense of humor. All things that made a person extremely attractive in her eyes.

Laura closed her eyes and took a deep breath. This train of thought wouldn't get her anywhere. Wyatt had already sacrificed enough for them without her needing to start crushing on him like a schoolgirl. He'd made no indication that he felt that way about her, and she couldn't make him uncomfortable by putting him in a position where he'd have to reject her romantically.

And what was wrong with her, anyway? Her husband had only been dead for four months, which made her thoughts seem all the more inappropriate.

Wyatt nodded deliberately, then turned his attention back to the road. "I didn't think about it until now, but this is your first rodeo since Cash's passing. It's really hard on you, isn't it?"

Great. Now, she'd made him feel bad, but for another reason.

"No, I hadn't given it much thought, but now that you mention it, it is going to be weird. I hadn't prepared myself for that. I've been so focused on the boys that I hadn't had the chance to think beyond that."

Wyatt looked over at her with an expression of deep sympathy. "It's going to be okay," he said. "We'll get through this. Between the lawyer we consulted, and the lady from child services, we had plenty of reassurance that the boys are safe from Cash's parents. They can't take the boys away from us."

Wyatt was trying to be nice, and she felt like a jerk because she was thinking about him in an inappropriate way, and his concern was strictly for the twins.

Yes, it was definitely wrong for her to be thinking along these lines. Especially since his train of thought was all about where it should be.

Wyatt glanced over at her once more. "Thank you again for being willing to come with me on this one. Even though Mike apologized, saying that Barbara was under a lot of strain over Cash's death, I just didn't feel right leaving you and the boys alone, not knowing what she was going to try next."

The look of concern on his face brought so much peace to her heart. Until Wyatt had come into her life in a more active away, she hadn't realized how little Cash had stood up to his parents on her behalf, and how much Wyatt did. She had never found fault with Cash as a husband, but more and more, she was seeing all the ways where he had let her down.

In a way, she was seeing Cash clearly for the first time. It made her wonder, was she so lost in the fantasy of her perfect marriage that she hadn't known her husband at all?

She'd always blindly trusted him, never looking below the surface or asking the deeper questions. Though she still felt betrayed by Cash, she was starting to see where she had made her own mistakes, like in not asking more questions about their money or expressing her frustration to him that he didn't defend her against his parents.

Maybe she and Wyatt didn't love each other in the way a couple should. But in the short time they'd been together, she'd come to see that they actually had a stronger relationship than she and Cash ever had. Even the simple conversations about Cash's parents would have never happened. Though she and Cash had talked all the time, these days, she couldn't remember what they talked about at all.

Wyatt glanced around the truck.

"What are you looking for?" she asked.

He sighed. "I went to all the effort to pack the cooler with snacks, and I forgot it on the porch."

Laura laughed. "No, you didn't. I had to pack stuff for the boys, so I redid it, then put it in the back with all of their stuff."

He grinned. "Could you grab me a drink and some sunflower seeds?"

A sad look crossed his face, then he smiled again. "It's been so long since we've been on the road together that we're going to have to get used to each other's routines again. Usually, about this time, Cash would've already broken out the sunflower seeds and we'd be chomping away."

She'd been wrapped up so much in her own grief and the mixed feelings she felt over her marriage, she'd forgotten that Wyatt was grieving, too. Cash had been his best friend, his traveling companion, and she and Wyatt had been so focused on all of the practicalities that she hadn't taken the time to check in on him emotionally.

"It must be hard for you, being on the road without him. Is there anything I can do to help with your grief?"

Giving him a moment to compose himself, she reached over the seat and moved the baby blanket covering the cooler to grab drinks for both of them as well as some snacks.

When she handed him his drink, he said, "Thank you. You do it, just like he did. You unscrewed the cap just enough so I don't have to fuss with it, but you leave it on so I can put it where I need it."

She shrugged. "You taught me that trick, back in the old days when we all traveled together."

One of the snacks she'd grabbed was some cheese she'd sliced up as well as crackers, and as she fixed one, she held it out to him. "Want one?"

The smile on his face warmed her heart. "I haven't had cheese and crackers on one of these trips since you stopped coming with us. Cash always said it was too much work."

Laura laughed. "I can see him saying that. I used to try to make snacks for him, but toward the end of my pregnancy, and once the boys were born, I didn't have the energy to do it anymore. I always felt bad about that."

Wyatt laughed, then said, "Don't let it trouble you too much. We might have missed out on the quality snacks, but Cash was happy to stop and get junk food when we got gas. I'm pretty sure he preferred the junk food."

Laura chuckled with him. "Oh yeah, he did. That used to be one of our running jokes. He was a junk food machine."

They sat in silence for a few minutes, then Wyatt said, "You asked me about my grief. And I don't have a simple answer. One minute, I'm mad as all get-out at him for all the secrets he held and the lies he told. But then the next minute, I miss him so much I can't breathe. Like that last trip on the road."

He glanced at her, then took a sip of his drink. "The truth is, I was glad for the excuse of bringing you and the boys with me. The last trip, being alone, was hard. I missed his dumb jokes, and pretty much everything, even his stinky feet."

The reference to Cash's stinky feet made Laura smile in spite of the somber mood.

They were the stuff of legend, and everyone liked to joke about it.

They were entering a curvy area, and Wyatt quieted again. But after he passed a semi going slowly up the hill, he continued. "I guess I haven't talked to you much about this, because I know you're dealing with your own pain. But just having said all this makes me feel better, and now I think we probably should have spoken of it sooner because we could've helped each other out. Yes, I want to protect the boys from Cash's parents. But the truth is, I was miserable on my own."

He gave her another quick glance. "I don't mean to put pressure on you by saying this, but I missed you. I missed the boys. I haven't felt right talking about how I miss Cash because it hasn't felt right to put the burden on you when you're already carrying so much. But this helps you just as much as it helps me, doesn't it?"

The vulnerability in his voice as he spoke touched her deeply. They'd never been this open with each other before. Which made sense, since they were never married before. She had never had the opportunity to get to know Wyatt on this deep level. Something about that brought a funny feeling to her stomach, and it made her aware of him in a new way. More so than when she'd been thinking she found him attractive.

She and Cash had taken for granted what they knew about each other. Maybe their easy and frequent conversations had fooled them into thinking they were communicating when they really weren't. Maybe, because they'd never gotten into the habit of sharing this deeply with each other, it was less that Cash was keeping secrets from her, and more that they'd simply never learned how to communicate properly.

Laura looked over at Wyatt. "Thank you for sharing all that with me," she said. "It just occurred to me that the real problem in my relationship with Cash is that we never talked about these things."

"It seemed like you guys talked about everything."

"That's what I thought too," she said. "But now I wonder how much of the problems I face now are because Cash and I never really talked."

She glanced back at the sleeping babies, feeling so much love in her heart. "I ranted to him all the time about how his mother upset me. But I don't think I ever just sat down with him and explained my deep hurt over how she treated me. For that matter, I never told his parents."

The understanding on his face comforted her. "He wasn't very good at that with me, either. I don't think any of us are."

Then he gave her a look that melted her heart. "But now that we recognize it, we can try to do better in our relationship."

Of all the times she had to remind herself that this wasn't a real marriage, this was probably the most important. Talking with Wyatt now, and seeing his willingness to make their relationship work, it created a longing in her for something more. Something she hadn't known she needed until now. She and Cash had thought that love was all that mattered, but now, she could understand the value of communication and being vulnerable, and mostly, being willing to work through whatever came up, even though it was hard.

"I can't tell you how much I appreciate this conversation," she said. "It's made me realize the areas that I would like to improve upon in our relationship."

His brow creased, and she wondered if she'd taken it too far.

"I didn't think of this as being a relationship," he said. "But you're right. Just because were not romantically involved doesn't mean we don't owe it to ourselves, and the boys, to have the best relationship we can."

What was he doing? Wyatt gripped the steering wheel tightly as he talked to Laura. She was right about their relationship in general. But he hadn't expected this to feel so much like a sucker punch. He hated talking about his grief with Laura because he didn't feel the same grief she did. Yes, he'd suffered the loss of a beloved friend. But for him, this was more than that. He'd caused his friend's death. He was the one who had to look himself in the mirror every morning and live with the knowledge that Cash's death was all his fault.

How do you grieve the person you killed? And how do you admit that fact to the woman grieving him? Some days, he didn't know how he could live with himself. Laura could talk about the mistakes in their relationship, but the thing was, if he hadn't killed Cash, she could have done all of these things to improve their relationship. There still would've been hope for their future. Wyatt had taken that from her.

Fortunately, Laura didn't feel the need to talk further, and she fell asleep shortly after, leaving him alone with his thoughts. He hadn't been lying when he said he'd been miserably lonely on his last trip. Even in the silence with Laura and the boys sleeping, he felt a strange sort of comfort.

Which was both heartening and disconcerting. In such a short time, he'd come to rely on Laura and the twins in ways he hadn't expected. They were becoming a real family, and while that had been the goal in a sense, it was doing things to Wyatt's heart he hadn't been prepared for.

Fortunately, the rest of the drive was uneventful. He'd booked them a hotel that was one of those residence suite places that he'd always thought too fancy for the likes of him, but it came with the bonus of not only having two bedrooms and a lounge area, but a nice little kitchenette where Laura could more easily handle preparations for the boys. But when they got to the room, instead of looking pleased at his forethought, she seemed upset.

"What's wrong?" he asked.

Laura sighed as she set Garrett's car seat

next to the couch. Wyatt set Cody's next to his brother.

"This seems awfully expensive," she said. "I know you keep saying that you have plenty of money, and I don't mean to call you a liar, but Cash had always told me that, too, and look where that got me."

She gestured around the room, her face filled with concern. "Maybe you can afford this now, but can you always afford a place like this? Will this dig in to the nest egg you say you've been saving?"

This was the first real test of their commitment to communication, and he was grateful it was an easy one. Hopefully, he could continue reassuring her so that the biggest secret he carried would not be one he would ever have to reveal.

Before he could answer, Garrett let out a wail. The babies had slept through most of the drive and when they'd been awake, they'd happily chattered and made baby noises. But with the gentle rocking of the truck gone, the little boys were looking around the room in confusion.

"I'm not dodging your question," he said. "Let's get the boys situated, the stuff brought in from the truck and then we can talk. I'll get out my laptop, and I'll go through all my finances with you."

His words didn't seem to erase the worry off her face, so he said, "I've only given you a small picture of my finances, so I can see where you're concerned. We should've gone over all of this sooner, and I'm sorry we haven't."

Finally, Laura seemed to relax. "That does sound good, thank you. I'm sorry that I seem like I don't trust you, but I made a mistake in not having all the information in my marriage to Cash, and I want to do better."

Was it wrong to be both happy and sad at her commitment? On one hand, this was exactly what every relationship needed. But on the other hand, it gave him a deeper glimpse into the amazing woman she was, and it made him long for something more.

Once the boys were happily settled, playing on blankets on the floor, Wyatt got his laptop out and set it up on the table. As he logged into the account, he said, "When we get home, I'll make sure you have all of my passwords. I know one of the things that was hard for you when Cash died was that you didn't have all of his, and you didn't know where all of his accounts were. I don't want you to be in that position again."

A deep sadness came over him as he remembered everything he and Laura had done to sort through Cash's financial mess. True, Cash had never expected that he'd die so soon, but he still should have been open with his wife.

Sharing this with Laura was the right decision, even though the mixture of pain and hope was obvious in her eyes. Though he wished he could take away the pain, knowing he could do better for her in the future made him even more confident in his decision. But it felt strange, as he logged on to his regular bank account and saw her eyes widen at the numbers.

"You and Cash made the same amount of money, didn't you?" she asked.

"About that," he said, feeling sick at how overwhelmed she must be, realizing just how much money he'd lost.

He'd wanted to save her from the pain of seeing the depth of betrayal, but in protecting her, he was doing the same thing.

"Actually, that's not true," Wyatt said. "Cash made a lot more than I did. He had more wins, including the championship, so it was a lot more money. I want to spare your feelings as much as I can, but I also don't want to keep you in the dark. So, you tell me. What else do you want to know?"

The tears in her eyes told him he'd said the right thing, even though it made him sick to once again face the amount of money Cash had squandered.

Garrett let out a wail as his brother hit him with a toy, and Laura went over to comfort him. Usually, she tried to let the boys figure these things out, but Wyatt could tell she needed space to process the information she'd been given.

As she sat on the floor with Garrett in her lap, Laura looked up at Wyatt. "I have moments when I wish I didn't know any of this, and I could pretend that Cash and I had the perfect life, but then I get mad because it was all a lie, and I want to know everything."

She gestured at his open laptop. "But then I see some of the truth and I feel incredibly stupid and naïve for being blind to it."

Wyatt came and sat next to her on the floor, and picked up Cody so the boys could play with each other in their laps. He'd have never imagined he'd find so much comfort holding a baby, but somehow, these little guys made this difficult conversation easier.

"You're the least stupid human being I know." He leaned forward and touched her arm. "In school, you were the smartest of all of us. You loved Cash, and you believed him."

Cody reached for one of the toys on the blanket, so Wyatt set him back down and let him play.

"If anyone was stupid, it was me," Wyatt admitted. "I believed Cash when he said he had things under control and was getting help. I believed all of his excuses and lies."

Garrett reached out to his brother, so Laura set him down, leaving her and Wyatt facing each other, baring their hearts about the pain Cash had caused.

"But you know, I don't think either of us was that stupid. We both loved Cash. Neither of us had reason to believe he was a liar. The mistakes we made, they were in the spirit of love. And now we know to do better."

Wyatt gestured at the computer and went to it again. Laura followed. "And that's why I'm doing this for you. Complete transparency on everything I can think of sharing with you."

Guilt nibbled at his insides as he spoke. He wasn't being completely transparent. Otherwise, he would just admit to her what he'd done. For the first time, Wyatt understood why Cash would keep all this from them.

The thought of losing Laura's regard tore at Wyatt's heart. Telling her the truth about his role in Cash's death would make her hate him.

Cash probably thought that's how everyone would react to his gambling addiction. But that was the difference between an addiction and causing someone's death. They would have all come around Cash to support him and help him. That wasn't possible in Wyatt's case.

So he'd do the best he could to be open with Laura about everything else, and pray that she would never find out the secret that kept him from loving her.

As they went through his accounts and he explained how he had been planning, he appreciated the knowledge and understanding in Laura's eyes. Wyatt had worked with a financial planner to invest his earnings wisely, knowing that his bronc riding career wouldn't last forever.

"This is really incredible," Laura said

when he was finally finished explaining everything to her. "I wish Cash had done the same. It seems like such a waste, knowing he earned all that money and I have nothing to show for it."

Seeing the pain in Laura's eyes made him feel even worse. "I'm sorry," he finally said. "I tried getting him to sit down with a financial adviser, but I always accepted his excuses. I feel like I let you down by not trying harder."

Laura shook her head. "None of this is your fault. You keep blaming yourself, saying you should have done more, but we both know how stubborn Cash was. Sure, you can advise him on things, but he has always been a man to make his own decisions."

Would she say that same impassioned thing, knowing that his negligence led to Cash's death?

"You don't understand all the mistakes I made," Wyatt said finally.

"So what?" She asked. "Don't you think we all have regrets?"

Laura got up from where they were sitting at the table and went to her overnight bag, then pulled something out of it.

He smiled as she paused at the boys, giving them each a loving pat. She was an incredible woman with such a loving heart.

When she came back, she set a Bible on the table. "Since Cash died, I have been reading this, searching for answers, trying to understand why."

"I've been doing the same," Wyatt admitted.

That's where he'd come up with this wild idea to marry her and take care of the boys. The whole caring for widows and orphans thing. But it seemed like, even though part of him knew it was the right thing to do, another part of him felt even more guilty for potentially ruining Laura's chances at happiness with someone else.

Laura leaned forward and squeezed his hand. "I know it's not a literal instruction manual, but it does comfort me, seeing all the mistakes we've made, and all the ways God has shown us love in spite of them."

She sighed sweetly, and his heart ached to hold her, to let her know that he understood, probably in an even deeper way.

"The thing about our mistakes," Laura continued, "is that we're given a choice. We can learn from them, or we can repeat them. I'm choosing to learn from mine."

She gestured at his still open laptop. “We should have had this discussion before we got married, but I’m glad we’re having it now. My mistake with Cash was not having this discussion, or any other discussion of substance. We took a lot about each other for granted, and never talked to each other about the things that mattered. Even though I think we had a good life together, I think about how much better it would have been if we had only discussed things like this.”

He didn’t say anything, because he didn’t have a response that would make her happy. None of Laura’s mistakes had been fatal. His had.

But it didn’t stop her from reaching forward and taking his hand in hers. “Nothing good has ever come out of beating yourself up for your mistakes. Yes, there are a million things you could have done differently, but we all know how stubborn Cash was. He would have still made his own decisions. We did our best, and that’s what matters.”

He accepted the comfort she gave, though he wanted to argue with her and tell her that it wasn’t as simple as she put it.

While he could accept that some of the things he felt guilty over were, in fact, Cash’s stubbornness, his death had been preventable. Sure, Cash had been insistent in his own way. But Wyatt knew he'd had a head injury, knew it was likely a concussion, and he should not have been driving. Cash wouldn't have had the mental capacity to make that realization, and that's where Wyatt had let him down. How many times had Wyatt taken the keys from a cowboy who'd had too much to drink to prevent a tragedy? This was no different, except in this case, Wyatt had failed to act.

Now he was failing to act again. As Laura talked of communication and openness, he longed to give her the depth she craved and tell her the secret burdening him. Every time he thought of how he'd contributed to Cash's death, he also remembered how desperate Barbara had been in trying to cause trouble for Laura. Telling the truth could add fuel to the fire in her desire to take the boys.

Wyatt was caught between his secret and his desire to do right by Laura, and he didn't know what to do.

Was there redemption for his sins? Technically, God forgave him, because Wyatt had asked for His forgiveness. He'd spent a great deal of time in prayer and reading the Bible, and he understood that God forgave your sins when you asked. But he wasn't so naïve as to believe that he didn't have to live with the consequences of those sins.

Garrett let out a belly laugh, drawing Wyatt's attention to the boys. They'd recently figured out how to pull off each other's socks, and now it seemed like they were making a game of it.

Who would have thought that a simple evening would feel so much like where he belonged.

Moments like these, the weight of what Wyatt had done felt a little bit lighter. Maybe there wouldn't be full redemption, but he could find contentment in simple things, and when Laura went over to blow raspberries on bare baby feet, Wyatt was overwhelmed with gratitude that God would see fit to give him these tiny blessings.

Even though Laura had balked at the idea of staying in a nicer hotel than what they were used to, the extra thirty dollars a night was more than worth the cost. The rest of the evening passed in contentment and ease as they alternated discussing finances and playing with the twins. The kitchenette allowed them to maintain the boys' routine as much as possible, and when they finally put them to bed in the porta cribs in Laura's room, he had never felt so much satisfaction.

All these years, Wyatt had been chasing dreams of championships, but no win he'd ever had felt quite this good.

Funny how quickly your priorities changed.

Laura closed the door behind her as she exited the babies' room, then walked into the kitchenette.

"I'm going to make myself a cup of tea and sit on the balcony for a bit. Would you like to join me?"

He should say no, because he always liked to get a good night's sleep before competition. You were only on the bronc for just a few seconds; however, all the waiting, the anticipation and adrenaline were exhausting. But the sweet smile on her face was hard to refuse.

"That sounds good. Did you bring that bedtime tea you like so much?"

Laura smiled at him, warming his insides more than any cup of tea. "Of course I did. I can't sleep without it."

Since they'd been together, Wyatt had also taken to her nightly habit, and he admitted that on evenings when they didn't share this ritual, he struggled going to sleep. He would have never imagined this life for himself. Sure, he'd thought that maybe someday he would have a family of his own, but that always seemed like a pipe dream further from his reach than the world championship. Yet here he was, and the thing he'd thought were the furthest was actually the nearest.

She made their tea and then they went out onto the balcony.

As much as he'd been hesitant to bring Laura and the boys with him on this trip, he was glad he had. From the balcony, they could look out across the area and to the fading light on the mountains in the distance. It was a beautiful calm evening, with the faint call of birds and crickets chirping, all signaling the end of the day. Though his habit was to spend the night before a rodeo relaxing as best as he could, he had never relaxed like this.

Usually, he and Cash would turn on some mindless television, talk about their plans, and when Cash went in to take a shower, Wyatt would use the time to pray and read his Bible.

Laura set her tea on the side table then said, "I'm feeling like something a little chocolatey. I'm pretty sure there were some brownies left. Do you want one?"

Wyatt shook his head. "No, thank you. I try not to have a lot of sugar before a ride, but feel free to enjoy yourself. Those were good brownies."

Wyatt had never been the kind of person to need someone to take care of him. He'd always known how to cook and clean, and everything else to take care of himself. Even though it hadn't been part of their agreement in getting married, Wyatt loved the way Laura cared for his needs. It wasn't one of those things she did out of obligation, but because she had such a good heart.

In the stillness of the evening, with Laura inside, he took advantage of the time to begin his prayer. Once he got settled in his bed, he'd likely pray some more, but in this beautiful, still evening, it felt right to give his heart to God.

Thank You, Lord, for giving me this blessing I don't feel I deserve, but You've chosen to give it to me anyway. I'm grateful for this moment to honor You, and to thank You for this amazing woman in my life, and these two beautiful boys. Please watch over us all. May Your hand of protection be on all of the cow-

boys, spectators and people assisting with the rodeo. Keep the animals safe. Help us all to do our jobs and to do them safely.

It was so still out, the air so peaceful, so Wyatt continued to pray. All the random thoughts, he turned over to God, and he found that the more he poured his heart out, the better he felt. All the weight he'd been carrying, all the guilt, it seemed to fall away, and all he felt was gratitude and love for the many blessings he had been receiving.

When he was finally finished, he realized that the sun had almost gone down, and his cup of tea that Laura had made him was getting cold. He turned in his seat. Where had she gone?

As if in answer, Laura came out the screen door.

"What took you so long?" he asked.

She gave him another one of those smiles that, as much as he tried to be immune to, melted him down to his toes.

"It seemed like you are having some really great prayer time with God, and I didn't want to mess it up. As hectic as our lives have been lately, I don't think any of us have had the opportunity to spend as much time with God as we'd like."

One more blessing to be thankful for. Not a lot of people understood the need for such intimate time with the Lord. That was one of the reasons why he hadn't had a relationship last all that long. Maybe it made him unusual, but he had always wanted a woman who had a deeper relationship with the Lord.

He patted the seat next to him. "There's a little bit of daylight remaining, and our tea is getting cold, so you might as well enjoy what's left."

She'd changed into a pair of flannel pajamas and was carrying a knitted blanket. Though the days were warm, sometimes the nights could be chilly, and he'd noticed that Laura always liked being warm and cozy. He didn't understand why, but knowing that about her, and seeing her in such a natural state made him feel closer to her. She sat in the chair and wrapped herself in the blanket, looking almost like a schoolgirl he remembered from years ago.

How was he not supposed to fall in love with her?

Brady's words about loving Laura echoed in his mind, and Wyatt did his best to dismiss them.

"This is my favorite time of night," Laura

said, sipping her tea. "You mentioned being lonely on the last trip, and I have to admit, I felt the same way. Sure, it was an intense weekend, and I missed your support, but it's more than that. I like that we sit together every evening, drinking tea, and enjoying each other's company."

Ouch.

That wasn't supposed to hurt, but this wasn't what he'd imagined when he had proposed marriage to Laura. Yes, he'd thought he would take care of her and the boys. And of course, they'd spend time together.

But needing each other like this?

"I like it, too," he admitted.

No. He wasn't supposed to do this. Yet baring his heart to Laura seemed like the most natural thing in the world.

Today had been too much, too risky. All the progress in their relationship made him feel like a failure in a sense that he wasn't protecting either of their hearts from potentially falling in love.

Laura deserved a better man than him, and he didn't deserve anything.

He certainly didn't deserve the tender smile she gave him as she reached out and took his hand.

"I'm really liking where our relationship is heading," she said. "You've given me more than I can ever imagine, and I hope you know just how much it means to me."

There were times when you were sitting on a bronc, and you knew things were going wrong, and the best thing you could do was bail. This felt like one of those times.

Wyatt pulled his hand from hers, picked up his cup of tea and drained it. "You know I'll always be here for you," he said.

Then he stood. "I need to get some rest for tomorrow. Good night."

Better to end a ride when it was reasonably safe, than stay on and risk injury.

It hurt to walk away, but sometimes, it was better than the alternative.

Chapter Eight

Her first rodeo in a year, and it seemed like nothing had changed. Laura walked through the back paddock, pushing the stroller toward where the contestants liked to hang out and chat. When Cash had insisted on getting the SUV of strollers for the twins, she'd thought he was being a little too extravagant.

"Nothing but the best of our boys," he'd said.

But now, even with all the financial heartache Cash had caused, Laura was grateful for the splurge. The stroller easily navigated the rocks, dirt and uneven terrain that came with the territory.

"Hey, little lady!" Tony Gill, one of the bronc riders who often vied for the top spot with Cash and Wyatt, greeted her warmly. "These must be our future cowboys."

She stopped to hug him, then stepped back to allow Tony to admire the boys, who were decked out in the cutest cowboy baby gear. Wyatt had bought them their tiny little cowboy boots as soon as she and Cash had told him they were expecting twin boys. The boots were still a little too big, but they were too adorable to not have the boys wear them.

"It's such a shame about Cash," Tony said, looking at her with sympathy. "I'm sorry I couldn't make the funeral."

"It's okay." She gave him a warm smile. "I was so upset that I don't remember who was and wasn't there."

"Tony!" Wyatt strode up to them and clapped his friend on his back. "Nice to see you."

"You, too," Tony said, then gave him a friendly punch in the arm. "You sly fox, you. Marrying the prettiest lady on the circuit before any of us got the chance to woo her."

Laura hadn't expected people to comment on their marriage so openly. But it was nice to at least get it out. Still, she hadn't thought much about what she'd say when people questioned them.

Wyatt came to stand beside Laura and put his arm around her waist. "I wasn't going to let her get away. She's pretty special, and..."

He gazed at her with such tenderness that she could almost believe he loved her.

It seemed to do the trick, because Tony chuckled. "Yeah, I guess none of us would have stood a chance anyway."

Then Tony looked down at the boys. "Plus, you got yourself a couple of cute rug rats. I've been thinking a lot about settling down and starting a family myself, so I can't say that I blame you. Cash's boys need a good man to raise them, and they'll have that with you."

Laura looked up at Wyatt and met his eyes. That was the one thing she had no doubt of. The boys would have a father who loved them and cared for them as his own. Even now, she could see the love he had for Garrett and Cody written all over his face. Though she'd connected with Wyatt on a deeper level last night, and Wyatt had turned away, she could push those thoughts aside as she reminded herself of the deeper, stronger love.

"I'll do my very best by them," Wyatt said solemnly.

Tony slapped him on the back. "Of course

you will. That's who you are. You always do your best. And why it's going to be so sweet today when I beat you."

They all laughed, and Laura felt relieved to have some of the pressure taken off of her discussing their relationship.

The truth was, she was starting to have feelings for Wyatt. Their every interaction was loving and supportive. Not in a romantic way, but how could you not develop romantic feelings for someone who cared about you so deeply? Wyatt had been working to ease her insecurities, help her feel stronger and give her the things she hadn't had in her marriage with Cash.

Ugh. This was not helping.

She was supposed to be thinking of non-romantic things, not reasons why she was developing feelings for him.

Fortunately, Gracie Calloway, who was married to another bronc rider the men often competed against, spotted them and came over.

"You brought the babies!" She squealed with delight and immediately bent down to inspect the boys. "They are so cute! I keep telling Harv that it's high time we started a family, and this just makes me want one even more. Can I hold one of them?"

How could Laura resist? She unbuckled Cody from his spot in the stroller and handed him to her friend. "This is Cody."

Once she got Cody situated in Grace's arms, Laura picked up Garrett. "And this is Garrett."

Wyatt immediately grabbed Garrett and cuddled him. "My little Gare-bear."

Gare-bear? She'd never heard him call her son that before, but at the way Wyatt and Garrett looked at each other, she couldn't think of anything more fitting. For whatever reason, Wyatt and Garrett had bonded the most strongly, and as much as Laura had always tried not to let anyone play favorites with the boys, she enjoyed how much the two seemed to love each other.

Harvey, Gracie's husband, strode up to them. "Oh, no you don't. Put that thing back where you got it." Though he sounded stern, there was a twinkle in his eyes.

"But he's so cute," Gracie said. "I want a baby so bad."

She snuggled Cody closer to her, and Harvey turned his attention from Wyatt to his wife. "If I win the championship, you can have your baby."

"Aw, that's no fair," Tony said. "She'll never get a baby that way. I'm winning it this year."

Wyatt squared his shoulders. "No, sir. That championship is mine. I'm winning it for my boys."

Instead of the good-natured laughing that always came with the men jockeying for the championship, everyone got quiet, until finally, Harvey said, "Yeah, I guess you've earned it."

Though Laura didn't expect Wyatt to jump for joy at the pronouncement, she was taken aback by the devastation on his face at his friend's comment.

"I never wanted it this way," Wyatt said softly, then handed the baby back to Laura. "I need to go check in."

Part of her wanted to go after him, to comfort him somehow. But he was walking fast, and she had a baby in her arms, with her other son being cooed at by her friend. Her responsibility was to her children, even if where she really wanted to be was comforting her husband.

"That was—" Tony looked at Harvey, then down at the ground.

"You shouldn't have said that, Harv." Gracie finally took her eyes off Cody to look at her husband. "I know we're trying to pretend that everything is normal, but Cash is dead, and we all loved him."

She kissed the top of Cody's head. "I'm sorry you won't get to know what a great man he was, little guy."

Laura's heart felt like it was going to break in two, and she didn't realize she had tears in her eyes until Gracie said, "Oh no. Now I've been the one to put my foot in it. I'm sorry, Laura. I was just trying to help."

Gracie held her hand out to Laura, and Laura took it and squeezed.

"It's okay. It's a hard situation, no matter how we look at it," Laura said. "But you know Cash. He'd have been here razzing all the guys, saying they can't beat him. He's not here to win it, so someone has to."

Harvey looked solemn. "Yeah, but none of us want the victory simply because Cash isn't here to take it."

That was probably why Wyatt had stormed off. He'd made enough comments about Cash not being here that she knew he carried a lot of guilt over Cash's death. She didn't know how to get through to him that none of this was his fault, and that of all people, Cash would be the happiest if Wyatt won.

"There's no guarantee Cash would have won this time, either. He won the championship because he drew a great bronc. Sure, it takes skill, and I'm not denying that Cash was good. But so are all of you. So is Wyatt. In the end, you do the best you can with what you've been given. You've all got the opportunity to win equally if you're looking at talent alone. Cash knew that. Winning isn't a given, which is why you all go out and give it your best, regardless of the bronc you draw."

Her words seemed to be what the men needed to hear. Even Gracie's face softened. "He was a great competitor. He used to make bets with some of the others on who would win. It was always so funny to watch."

Gracie's mention of the word *bet* made the other men look uncomfortable, and Laura's stomach hurt. Did everyone know about Cash's gambling problem except her?

"What?" Gracie asked. "I mean, sure, he owed Harv a couple hundred bucks after that last rodeo, but we knew he'd be good for it eventually. It was no big deal."

How had Laura not known this about her own husband?

"I'm sorry. If you let me know how much, I'll make sure you're repaid," Laura said quietly.

Harvey shook his head. "Don't worry about it. Honestly, I'd forgotten about it until now."

He gave his wife a look as if to tell her not to say anything else, and that's when it hit her just how much Cash had lied to her.

"You all knew he had a gambling problem, didn't you?" Laura asked.

"He said he could handle it," Harvey said.

Tony shook his head. "But we also all knew better than to lend him money or make a bet with him. What were you thinking?"

"Why didn't anyone tell me?" Laura asked. "I feel like I'm learning so much about him now that he's gone, but I feel like I never really knew him at all."

Gracie touched her arm. "Of course you knew him. Everything you just said about him as a competitor and how he saw the game was exactly who he was. But he couldn't resist a good bet, and while it caused problems for him, it didn't mean he didn't love you. I think he thought he was protecting you."

Protecting her? That's not what Laura would have called it. Yet it didn't do her, or anyone else, any good to play the blame game. But it didn't change the hurt she felt, realizing that everyone here had known all along.

"I suppose it doesn't matter," Laura said. "But it does make me wonder, who else does he owe money to? Has he hurt any of our other friends because of this money situation?"

Gracie touched her arm gently again. "Not at all. Like Harv said, he knew what he was getting into. We all loved and cared about Cash, despite the finances. Everyone knew that if they didn't want to lose their money, not to give it to Cash."

While Laura understood this was supposed to make her feel better, it only made her feel worse. It just highlighted that a problem clear to everybody else was a complete mystery to the woman he'd married.

While she'd been talking, Cody had wiggled in her friend's grasp enough to reach forward and pull a lock of Gracie's hair.

"Ouch." Gracie jumped, and Cody laughed.

Gracie started laughing with him as she brushed her hair away from his wandering hand. "I forgot how much babies like to pull hair," she said.

Laura chuckled. "Sorry, I wasn't paying attention. Otherwise I'd have warned you. That's why I always keep mine pulled back. Otherwise, I'd probably be bald by now."

Gracie laughed, and the tension of dealing with the painful past dissipated.

The men must've thought so, too, because they looked at each other, then Tony said, "We should probably head over to registration as well."

Once they left, Gracie said, "I'm really sorry if I opened wounds for you. I didn't mean to, and I honestly didn't think before I said anything. Please forgive me if I caused you any pain."

Even though Laura's feelings were hurt that her friends hadn't told her about Cash's problem, it also wasn't their responsibility. As a wife, she should have been paying more attention to things like their finances. She should have noticed that her husband had a problem.

"It's not your fault," Laura said. "I just feel so stupid that I didn't know. I feel like in some ways, my marriage was a lie."

Gracie shifted the baby in her arms and gave Laura an awkward side hug. "Never say that. The one thing all of us knew was how much Cash loved you. I think that's why he kept this from you. That's why we all did."

Love wasn't about keeping secrets, but telling Gracie that wasn't going to change anything. Laura looked around and saw the activity in the area picking up, realizing that things were about to kick off. She put Garrett in his seat and strapped him in, then reached for Cody. "I guess we better go find some seats," she said.

"Thank you for letting me have time cuddling your baby. If you ever want help with them, let me know. I'm glad to help out. I'm loving getting a baby fix."

On her way to the seat, Laura ran into a number of old friends, and it warmed her heart to see all the support she was being given. Going home to Shepherd's Creek had been the right choice in returning to her family, but being here, at the rodeo, it was like being with yet another family. Having all this support meant the world to Laura, and it made her realize just how blessed she was to be part of it.

Bringing twin babies to a rodeo was not for the faint of heart. The boys were getting to the age where the last thing they wanted to do was be cooped up in their stroller all day. Laura found herself playing the "pick up the toy they threw from the stroller" game ad nauseam.

She'd never imagined she'd be at a rodeo without Cash, and yet, she didn't miss him nearly as much as she'd thought she would. True, even when he'd been here, she hadn't seen him much, since he was usually running around, helping his friends, but she'd gotten little glimpses of him that always made her heart race.

Now she was looking for a different cowboy, and though she wouldn't say it was quite the same feeling she'd had with Cash, she felt better every time she spotted Wyatt. The sight of Wyatt standing near the chutes or helping one of his buddies made her feel warm inside, a gentle glow that gave her comfort.

"Laura!" An older woman stopped near Laura's seat. "I'm Pattie Lou Washington. I followed your husband on the circuit."

Laura smiled at Pattie Lou. "Of course. How could I forget? You made the loveliest baby blankets for the boys."

Pattie Lou beamed with pride, and once again, Laura felt incredibly blessed to have so many wonderful people in their lives. The older woman bent in front of the stroller. "May I?"

"Of course," Laura said. Pattie Lou bent down and made baby noises at the boys, which caused them to giggle. It made Laura feel like it had been the right decision to bring her sons, seeing just how many people loved them.

By the time the bronc riding started, enough people had come by to say hello and meet the twins that it felt like Laura had never been away.

However, when they announced the lineup, Laura's heart sank. Wyatt was going to be riding Daddy's Little Nightmare, one of the toughest broncs in the circuit.

Usually, an experienced cowboy knew the different horses well enough that they could reasonably predict how the animals were going to come out of the chute and how they would behave. Not so with Daddy's Little Nightmare. He was the most unpredictable horse Laura had ever seen, and while most of the guys liked a challenge, they all dreaded drawing this one. Most couldn't stay on him long enough to get a score, let alone a good one.

When Wyatt's turn came up, Laura said

a prayer, then held her breath. After all the excitement, the boys were sleeping in their stroller. How they could sleep through this, she didn't know, but she was grateful that she didn't have to worry about watching them and could focus on her husband's ride.

The horse came bursting out of the chute, then was spinning wildly. He turned to the left, then to the right, then back left again. Wyatt clung to the horse, in perfect position, his arm held high as he spurred Daddy's Little Nightmare on.

No one would have guessed this was the horse everyone dreaded having to ride with the way Wyatt handled him. It was like watching a master class on the perfect ride. The crowd roared with every twist of the horse, every kick from Wyatt's legs. When the buzzer sounded, Laura couldn't believe it had only been eight seconds. It felt like a lifetime, and for every single moment she'd watched her husband ride, it was as if he owned that horse.

Wyatt jumped off the horse and gave a fist pump to the cheering crowd. This was, hands-down, the best ride Laura had ever seen, and by the crowd's reaction, they felt the same way.

When the announcer shared Wyatt's score, it came as no surprise that this was the highest of the rodeo.

Overjoyed at Wyatt's performance, Laura gathered up her things and pushed the stroller to the area where she could meet Wyatt and congratulate him on a job well done.

On her way to the paddock, people stopped her to tell her how amazing that ride was, and she couldn't agree more. She'd watched Cash win so many times, and even Wyatt a few times, but this felt more special than any of the others.

Laura was just as full of adrenaline as she'd have been had she won it herself when she finally found Wyatt, who was surrounded by so many of their friends. They all knew he'd won it, and even though they were slightly disappointed at having not done so themselves, having seen Wyatt triumph on the unwinnable horse was victory enough.

"Wyatt!" Laura called, and she smiled as he turned his attention to her.

He ran over to her and lifted her off the ground, before spinning her around.

"That was amazing," she said, her heart full of joy.

"Best feeling ever," Wyatt said, setting her down. "Thank you for being here."

The light shining in his eyes was one of the most beautiful sights she'd ever seen.

"Always," she said, and this time, when he picked her up and spun her around, he kissed her before setting her down.

The press of Wyatt's lips against hers wasn't the fleeting tentative touch their wedding kiss had been, but this one shook her just as soundly.

His lips were soft, but firm, and even though the kiss lasted but a moment, she could feel the strength in him.

Laura kissed him back, and he pulled her closer to him. But as she sighed with contentment, a wolf whistle from somewhere in the crowd interrupted the moment. Wyatt stopped abruptly and pulled away, staring at her.

"Wyatt—" she started to say, but he shook his head.

"Don't," he said.

Then, without another word, he turned and strode away.

Not that he got far with all the well-wishers stopping him to congratulate him and cheer him on. She could have caught up with him, but it would have been useless to have a conversation with him, given all the excitement.

Wyatt glanced back at her, and the expression on his face broke her heart. He'd gone from being elated to looking like someone had just told him his score no longer counted.

What had just happened?

Wyatt sat in the corner of the restaurant, his hat pulled down low to discourage anyone from coming to talk to him. Today had been a disaster.

Yes, he'd won. The best win of his career. On a horse neither he nor Cash had ever been able to stay on.

And then the unthinkable had happened.

Why had he gone and done such a stupid thing as kiss Laura?

He dipped a fry in ketchup and ate it slowly. It had taken him almost two hours to get through his meal of a burger and fries, and he was almost out of time. He'd told Laura he was going out to celebrate and wouldn't be back at the hotel until late.

But listening to the congratulations, along with the comments about the kiss, had been too much to handle. He left the place where everyone usually hung out, and found himself sitting in this random restaurant, hiding in a corner, not sure how he was going to face what he'd done.

He pulled out his phone and stared at it. At the very least, he needed to let Laura know he was safe.

All the unread texts and voice mails stared back at him, calling him a coward. This should have been the biggest celebration of his life, yet here he was, hiding from the fact that, in his excitement, he'd gone and ruined everything.

"Hey, cowboy." Laura slid into the booth next to him.

Wyatt stared at her. "What are you doing here? Where are the boys?"

She gave him the kind of smile that should have melted him, but only made him feel sick.

"Gracie offered to sit with them in our hotel for a while. She's hoping to convince Harvey that if they can manage two of ours for an evening, one of theirs won't be so bad."

She signaled the waitress, who stopped at the table. "Would you mind bringing me your most decadent dessert, two spoons and two coffees?"

When she left, Wyatt said, "I don't need anything."

"Hush," Laura said. "I am fully prepared to eat the entire dessert myself, but at some point, you're going to want a bite, and then you'll need coffee to wash it down, so we might as well be ready."

Then her voice took a more serious tone. "As for your other question, Tony saw you headed in here. He tried to call you to ask you to join them, but he said you weren't answering your phone. Since you were dodging my calls, and you were gone longer than I would have expected, I figured I'd come see what's going on."

Laura leaned forward on the table. "So. What's going on?"

He'd just promised to communicate with her, just over twenty four hours ago, and yet, he couldn't find the words to explain how he felt.

The kiss had been amazing. And devastating.

It had been obvious, from the way she'd responded to him, that she'd enjoyed the kiss, too.

By the way she stared at him expectantly, she wasn't going to let him off the hook, either.

Laura wanted answers, and while he knew he owed her an explanation, he didn't know what to say.

The waitress brought the dessert and coffee, and Laura dug in like she'd found paradise. Which, were he in a better mood, he might have felt the same way. The rich chocolate cake was topped with ice cream, along with hot fudge, whipped cream, sprinkles and a cherry. When she took her first bite, the expression of bliss on her face made him wish he hadn't been so stubborn. Especially since a bit of the fudge remained on her lip, reminding him of what he really wanted, but couldn't have.

"I broke my promise," he finally said.

Laura set her spoon down. "What do you mean?"

"I told you it would be a marriage in name only, and then I went and kissed you. I'm sorry. It won't happen again."

There. He said it. Maybe it wasn't the most eloquent speech, but he'd gotten it out without choking on his words. What did you call a lie that had to be the truth? He wasn't sorry for kissing her, except that he knew he shouldn't have.

"Maybe we need to rethink the terms of

our marriage," Laura said quietly. "It takes two to kiss, and I kissed you back."

Wyatt shook his head. "It's just the adrenaline talking. Not love."

"No." The disbelief in Laura's eyes tore at his heart. "There are real feelings between us. Last night..."

She trailed off, then sat silently for a moment as she said, "I had the feelings last night, but you didn't, did you? That's why you left. You were trying to spare my feelings."

A tear rolled down her cheek, and more than anything, Wyatt wanted to wipe it away, take her in his arms and tell her she was wrong.

He'd felt the connection last night, too. Worse, he'd been tempted to kiss her then, but he'd done the honorable thing and walked away.

But it was better to say nothing, and let her believe what she believed than to admit that he was falling for her, too.

If Laura ever learned the truth, she'd look at him with disgust, not love.

"I'm sorry," he said again.

And truly, he was. When they were discussing marriage, they'd both agreed to set each other free should one find love elsewhere. But the great tragedy of Wyatt's life was that the only woman he could possibly imagine himself loving was sitting right next to him, and he could never have her.

Another tear trickled down her cheek. "I've made a mess of things, haven't I? I thought we'd connected, but..."

More tears now, and Wyatt hated seeing them. But he took every single one of them as the punishment he deserved.

She took a drink of her coffee, then looked up at him. "Did I ruin everything between us?"

Wyatt shook his head. "No, of course not. But I needed to create space between us, so that—"

"So I didn't get carried away in another fantasy," Laura finished for him. "I get it."

Laura stared at the dessert in front of her. "I guess it's just me and the one true love who will never let me down. Chocolate."

Could she pour it on any thicker? It was taking every ounce of strength he had not to give in to the emotions he was fighting.

"I won't let you down, either," Wyatt said. "At least not in the ways I've promised you. I just can't give you...that."

Laura looked at him thoughtfully. "Is there someone else? Because we promised each other that we'd set each other free if we met someone. Your happiness means the world to me, and I won't keep you tied down if there's someone you want to be with."

This was exactly why he hadn't wanted to have this conversation. Poor Laura was overanalyzing and he couldn't give her what she really wanted to hear.

"No," he said honestly. "Please, just let this be. Let's go back to where we were before the kiss, and work on remaining friends, okay?"

For a few minutes, Laura focused on her dessert with the same single-minded attention he gave the broncs. He forced himself not to look at her, because her strained expression tore at his will.

Once again, she set her spoon down and looked at him. "This is about Cash, isn't it?"

That was the trouble with knowing someone for as long as he'd known Laura. She understood him better than anyone, and after all their talks, it wasn't hard to guess his priorities. Which was why he had to protect himself, and her, from the truth.

Wyatt picked up the extra spoon and dug into the dessert. She hadn't been wrong about him eventually wanting a bite. At least with his mouth full, he couldn't tell her all the things on his heart.

"I get it," Laura said. "Don't you think I feel weird, having feelings for Cash's best friend? But what we have is different from what Cash and I had. He always said that he just wanted me to be happy, and that if something ever happened to him, I shouldn't hesitate in finding someone else to love. So here I am, not hesitating."

Didn't every man wish for the woman he loved to give such an impassioned speech?

"I'm sure he didn't mean with me," Wyatt said quietly.

Cash had asked him to take care of Laura and the boys, not take over his life. Certainly not after having been responsible for ending it.

"Why not with you?" Laura asked. "Cash trusted you above all others. I would think that if he'd had to pick my next husband, he'd have chosen you."

Had it not been for Laura's reminder of Cash's trust in him, he might have almost bought her argument. But that was just it. Cash trusted him, and Wyatt had let him down.

"This conversation is pointless. I don't

want to hurt you, but I'm not willing to have anything more than friendship with you. So please, for the sake of our continued good relationship, can we drop this?"

Wyatt hated breaking her heart like this, especially since he'd been the one to get her hopes up in the first place by kissing her. But better now, with this minor conflict, than spending a lifetime loving her only to destroy her with the truth.

"All right." Laura's voice cracked, like she was trying not to cry. "You've done so much for us, and the least I can do to repay you is not to burden you with these unwelcome feelings. I'm sorry I misinterpreted things."

"It's okay."

He wanted to take her hand in his, to give her some comfort, but touching her was too dangerous for both of them.

"I'm sorry I couldn't give you what you wanted."

"I'll be fine," Laura said. "I should get back to the boys. I don't want to impose on Gracie too much. Besides, if both babies start crying at once, she'll never convince Harvey to start a family."

Though Wyatt had dated before, he'd never experienced the feeling of a broken heart.

He'd counseled enough friends through it to know this was what he was feeling. The only difference was, instead of some woman doing him wrong, he'd done this to himself.

But having taken everything else from Cash, Wyatt simply couldn't bring himself to take his wife. Nor could he risk hurting Laura even more if she ever found out the truth.

Chapter Nine

Wyatt had asked that they go back to the way things were before the kiss, but Laura hadn't figured out a way to do so. Neither, it seemed, could he. They both acted like polite roommates, and even their nightly tea habit had returned to just Laura, sitting alone with her tea and her book.

Even though she'd felt guilty for her impulse buy at the drugstore, she was now grateful for something to distract her in the evenings, to help her forget that this used to be her special time with Wyatt.

This was their third rodeo since Wyatt's big win, and he'd won the others since. His current standings had him qualified for the world championship, so at this point, the rodeos he competed in were just gravy. His rides kept getting better and better, and by some unspoken agreement, Laura hadn't gone down to congratulate him, but instead, went back to the hotel room to wait for his return, which was when she'd politely tell him he'd done a good job.

A knock sounded at the door. Laura set her book down and got up to answer it. Wyatt probably forgot his key. He and a few of the guys had gone out for dinner, kind of a guys' night thing, leaving Laura and the boys to a quiet evening at the hotel.

However, when Laura answered it, the Fishers stood at the door.

"Can we come in?" Mike asked.

Though Laura and Wyatt had agreed that Laura wouldn't meet with the Fishers alone, they'd had several cordial video chats since the child services incident. Everyone had agreed it would be best for the Fishers to return to Texas for a while to give the families time to calm down.

This was the first rodeo they'd been to in Texas since Laura started traveling with Wyatt, so it was no surprise that they'd see the Fishers here, though Laura hadn't expected them to show up at the hotel.

"How did you know where we were staying?" Laura asked.

Wyatt stepped in behind them. "Sorry, I was going to call you to let you know they were coming, but my phone died right after I talked to them, and I forgot my charger. I'd hoped to beat them here, but..."

He gave a small shrug, then said, "I didn't think there'd be any harm in letting them have a quick visit with the boys."

"I just got them down to sleep," Laura said. Then she gestured into the room. "But I'm happy for you to come in for some tea and a chat. You're welcome to sit with me tomorrow at the rodeo and you can play with them then."

Barbara looked like she was going to argue, but Mike smiled and said, "That would be great, thank you. We haven't been to a rodeo since before Cash..."

The grief in the older man's voice tore at her heart. This was why, despite the fact that her lawyer had said she didn't owe the Fishers anything, least of all time with her sons, she was willing to keep trying.

"If you would prefer not to go, we could meet for breakfast tomorrow," Laura said, trying to give them a way to meet in the middle.

"I can't," Wyatt said. "I promised the Rodeo Network I'd be there early to film a segment for them."

On the drive here, Wyatt had shared his excitement over the possibility of being part of a special they were doing on the top bronc riders in the nation. As part of the special, they were going to do a tribute to Cash.

"Is that for the tribute to Cash?" Barbara asked.

The happiness in the older woman's voice brought peace to Laura's heart. It seemed like Barbara was finally finding comfort after Cash's death.

Wyatt nodded. "Yes. They're doing a whole series on bareback bronc riders. I'm excited to talk about Cash and the impact he had on the sport. He meant a lot to a lot of people, and it feels good to honor him this way."

"Before he died, they had asked him to host the show as the current world champion," Barbara said slowly. "He was going to interview his heroes."

Laura hadn't known that, and it made her a little sad that Cash hadn't told her about something so exciting. But more and more, it felt like she'd been married to a stranger. Something she'd hoped to avoid with Wyatt, but that kiss had changed everything between them.

She noticed that Wyatt didn't mention that they were also featuring him, and he'd seemed strangely embarrassed about that fact. But it wasn't Laura's place to question him on it, not anymore. It was like a wall had come up between them, and so many personal topics were off-limits.

Garrett started crying in the other room. Unusual for him, since both boys had been sleeping through the night for quite some time, and they'd taken to life on the road like champions.

But at least this would give Barbara and Mike some time with her son.

"I'll be right back," Laura said.

When she entered the room, she could see what had woken up the baby. He'd rolled over in his sleep and kicked one of the supports, collapsing it on top of him. Which shouldn't have happened.

Laura picked Garrett up and held him close to her. "Sorry, little guy. I'll get your daddy to fix it."

He whimpered in her arms and looked up at her like she'd let him down somehow.

She carried him into the other room and held him out to Barbara. "I think he had a bad dream or something. Do you want to hold him until he falls back asleep?"

Wyatt looked at Laura like he knew something was wrong. She shook her head slightly, not wanting to let the Fishers know what had happened.

As Barbara took the baby, she sniffed. "He needs to be changed."

All the diapers and baby gear were in the bedroom, so Laura turned back. "I'll just get what we need."

But rather than letting Laura do it, Barbara followed her. She immediately noticed the porta crib.

"What happened here?" she demanded.

The noise woke Cody, who started crying as well. Laura picked him up and cradled him. "It's okay, buddy."

"It is not okay," Barbara said. "My grandson was sleeping in a broken bed."

Wyatt entered the room, flanked by Mike.

"I was going to have you take a look at it before putting Garrett back to sleep," Laura told Wyatt, explaining what she thought had happened.

Wyatt examined the porta crib. "Oh man. I totally missed this setting it up."

He pointed out one of the locking pins. "It's broken. It must have happened when I dropped it, getting it out of the truck. I'll call the front desk and see if they have one we can borrow for the night, and you can get a new one tomorrow."

Wyatt reached over patted Garrett gently. "Daddy's sorry, Gare-bear."

Though it warmed Laura's heart to see the deep love Wyatt had for Garrett, Barbara flinched. They hadn't told the Fishers that they'd decided that the boys would call Wyatt Dad, and Laura felt bad they'd found out this way.

"Daddy?" Barbara asked.

Laura took a deep breath. "Cash will always be their father, and we're going to raise them so they know that. But Wyatt is also their father, and it's easier for them to call him that."

Bracing herself for a fight, she looked over at Wyatt, whose face had darkened.

"I see," Barbara said.

Then Mike held out his arms. "Any chance

I can hold Cody for a while? Let's get these boys some fresh diapers and get them back to sleep."

God bless Mike and his diplomacy. They definitely should have planned on telling Mike and Barbara in a better way, but at least it was over with.

Laura handed Cody to him. "That sounds like a great idea."

After changing the babies, everyone went into the other room while Wyatt called the front desk and made arrangements for a porta crib to be brought up. While most hotels had them available, they'd always brought their own, since they required two.

Once they were settled back in the other room, Barbara seemed to forget the tension over the porta crib and calling Wyatt Daddy, as she rocked Garrett back to sleep. The look of love on her face reminded Laura that despite her personal differences with the Fishers, the boys needed the love of their grandparents. Laura hadn't grown up with them, and she'd always been envious of her friends who had relationships with theirs.

Even though Laura kept Mike and Barbara informed of the boys' progress through regular video chats, they still had a million questions about the twins, and it felt good to share how well they were growing.

"It's a shame we'll be at the rodeo all day tomorrow, because the boys have started creeping a little, and I'd love for you to see it. They'll be crawling at any time." Laura laughed. "Though I'm not sure how I'm going to keep track of them once they're fully mobile."

Wyatt came back into the room and put his hand on Laura's shoulder. "You'll do just fine. Everything is babyproofed, and I've never seen a more attentive mother."

He looked pointedly at Barbara when he complimented Laura's mothering skills.

"I'm just sad we'll miss it," Barbara said, looking put out.

"Now, now," Mike said. "I'm retiring soon, and then we can move to Colorado, where you'll get to see the boys more often."

Retiring? Moving? This was the first Laura had heard this, though she knew Barbara had been intending to move to Colorado as soon as possible.

Having them in Texas had been a nice break for Laura, and she'd hoped Mike's job would keep them there for the foreseeable future.

"And in the meantime, I'll still keep sending you videos," Laura said. "I get my camera at the ready every time one of them does the rocking thing. I'm always nervous that they'll crawl for the first time when Wyatt is working in the stables instead of when he's home for the evening."

Laura hoped she sounded encouraging, like she was doing her best to accommodate Barbara, but as usual, Barbara looked unhappy.

"It's not the same as seeing it in person."

Laura took a deep breath and said another silent prayer for patience.

"Now, hon, Laura was just saying that not even Wyatt is guaranteed to see it in person." Mike laughed. "And once they start, everyone will probably be wishing the boys had taken it a little more slowly. I remember when Cash was that age. He got into everything. Do you remember how he got into the cat's food and ate it?"

The way the older man's face crinkled up as he smiled warmed Laura's heart.

"Don't remind me," Barbara said. "It was disgusting. Every time I turned around, I had to drag him away from the cat's food and water."

Instead of agreeing with her, Mike laughed even harder, then turned to Laura. "Did we ever tell you about how he thought he was a cat? At least until he discovered horses. Then he wanted to ride everything like a horse, including the cat. I think he was born to ride. It's all he ever wanted to do."

"I never heard the cat part," Laura said. "But I still have the picture of him as a toddler, riding Mike like a horse."

As they reminisced about Cash's early years, the boys fell asleep. Everyone, including Barbara, seemed to have relaxed. It was almost like they were a real family. When the hotel staff member arrived with the porta crib, Laura almost hated the interruption.

Maybe there was hope for them after all.

Once they got everything set up and the boys tucked in, Wyatt addressed the Fishers. "I hate to cut our evening short, but I like to get to bed early the night before a rodeo. I hope we'll see you tomorrow."

After Laura made arrangements to meet up with them in the morning, the Fishers left, and Wyatt went to bed in his room. While she wished they could have stayed up to chat and process the evening, Laura knew how important it was for Wyatt to get some sleep.

As it was, it was an hour later than what he usually preferred. Still, she wished she could have gotten some insight into how he was feeling, because he seemed quieter than usual. Distracted. Hopefully, some time in prayer and a good night's sleep would put him in a better place.

The next day, Laura was filled with more hope than she'd had in a long time. Not only did it seem like she and the Fishers had turned a positive corner in their relationship, but Abigail was flying out to watch the rodeo with her. She'd have driven out with them, but she was working to get her degree in child psychology and had an exam she couldn't miss. Over the years, Abigail had been taking a few online classes here and there, but with Josie's return, and now Laura's, everyone had encouraged her to take the plunge to be a full-time student, since she was just a few credits from finally getting her degree.

Laura couldn't be more proud of her sister for finally having the chance to follow her dreams. Abigail had supported her so much over the years, and even now, she'd found a way to make it work to be here for Laura.

Wyatt might not be available for emotional support, but at least Laura had her sister.

By the time Laura had picked up Abigail and they'd arrived at the arena, things were starting to get rolling. The music blared over the speakers, filling Laura with the energy that always came with being at a rodeo.

They took their seats, but the Fishers hadn't arrived yet. Gracie spotted Laura immediately, and came running over.

"There's my favorite boys!" she squealed. "Gimme, gimme, gimme!"

Though Gracie said this was her baby fix, Laura had a feeling that Gracie would be here this time next year with a baby of her own.

As she always did, Laura took the boys out, and gave one to Gracie. This time, it was Garrett. She held Cody out to Abigail. "Want a turn?"

"Yes!" Abigail nuzzled Cody as she grabbed him, and the little boy laughed with joy.

Having her boys surrounded with so much love was the biggest blessing Laura could have imagined.

The rodeo got underway, and soon Laura was lost in the usual routine, alternating between watching events, catching up with friends and playing pass the babies.

When Mike and Barbara finally arrived, Barbara looked more put out than usual.

"Who are all these people with my grandsons?" she demanded. "They could be spreading germs."

Laura glanced over at Abigail, who rolled her eyes. Gracie was holding Cody, talking to him and pointing out something. Pattie Lou, who had also become a good friend, had Garrett in her lap, letting him play with the yarn from her latest knitting project.

"They are both very good friends who I trust. They're in good health and are conscientious about not spreading germs. The last rodeo, Pattie Lou wasn't feeling well, so she didn't come."

At the mention of her name, Pattie Lou turned to them. "Hi, I'm Pattie Lou Washington, and you must be Cash's parents. I've heard so much about you."

She gestured at the arena. "My son is Ricky Washington, and his turn is in a few minutes."

Pattie Lou leaned down to Garrett. "Now don't you go and be stupid like my boy and take up steer wrestling."

The rest of the people in their section laughed. They often debated with Pattie Lou about which was the safest rodeo event, and even though Pattie Lou was her son's biggest supporter, she made no secret of her desire for her son to do something less dangerous.

Something she had in common with Barbara. Maybe the women could become friends.

Laura introduced the Fishers around, but Barbara didn't look any more comfortable.

"Okay, ladies, let's give the grandparents a chance to hold the boys. After all, that's what they're here for," Laura said, hoping Barbara would appreciate the gesture.

When Gracie handed Cody to Barbara, Barbara made a noise. "He's filthy."

"We're at a dusty arena," Laura said, reaching into the baby bag for some wipes. "Feel free to clean him up, even though he'll be coated in dust again in another few minutes."

Pattie Lou handed Garrett to Mike. "A little dirt never hurt anyone. In fact, I'm convinced that it helps build their immune system."

The horrified look on Barbara's face told Laura that her idea of Barbara and Pattie Lou becoming friends might not work out as Laura hoped. But that was okay. What mattered was that the Fishers were getting time with the boys, and Laura was surrounded by people who supported them.

As the rodeo continued, Barbara seemed to settle in. It probably helped that she had a squirming baby in her lap, and it took all of her energy to keep him occupied. As the boys grew, Laura was even more grateful for their rodeo family, helping her corral them while they were here.

Finally, Wyatt was up. On Killer Klown, a crowd favorite, though Laura didn't like the way he always made a hard left turn immediately after coming out of the chute. Wyatt tended not to favor that side, and often had difficulty maintaining position when the broncs did that. Fortunately, Wyatt was probably aware of that and would compensate, but it didn't stop Laura from saying a prayer and holding her breath as the horse exited the chute.

However, instead of his usual hard left, Killer Klown went right, then twisted back to the left in a move that Wyatt clearly wasn't prepared for. Laura's heart leaped into her throat as Wyatt came flying over the top of the horse, twisting in the air as he tried to get his bearings to land safely. But Wyatt was too close to the fence, and when he came down, his head hit the railing.

Adrenaline rushing through her body, Laura jumped up and turned to Barbara and Abigail. "Can you two take charge of the boys so I can check on Wyatt? That looked like a bad one."

She tried to sound calm, but her chest was pounding. Bad one didn't even begin to describe the fears racing through her mind. Every worst-case scenario flashed in her head, and the only thing she could do was pray, "Please, God."

"Of course," Barbara said. "You can count on me."

As Laura raced toward the first-aid area, Mike was on her heels.

"You don't have to come," Laura said. "Stay and help Barbara with the boys."

"No. Wyatt is like a second son to me. I can't lose him, too." The pain in the older man's voice made Laura's heart ache.

She hadn't thought about losing Wyatt until now, and the idea terrified her.

Though Wyatt had made his position on their marriage clear, once she knew he was okay, Laura was going to try harder to convince him that they needed to have a real marriage. The time they had together was precious, and no one knew how long they had. She wanted to take advantage of whatever time God gave them.

Whether he liked it or not, Laura loved Wyatt, and she was tired of denying it.

The medic at the first-aid stand knew Laura, and let them pass.

Wyatt lay on a gurney, muttering incoherently.

"Is he going to be okay?" Laura asked, trying not to betray the panic she felt. Staying calm was the best thing she could do in this situation, and it seemed like a monumental task to hold back the tears that were threating to spill out.

One of the paramedics turned and looked at her. "Definitely a concussion, but we need to get him to the hospital to assess the extent of his head injury."

As Laura stepped back to let the paramedics do their thing, Wyatt tried to sit up, seemingly recognizing Mike. Or so Laura thought until he spoke.

"Cash," Wyatt said. "I'm so sorry."

Everyone said that Cash was the spitting image of Mike when he was younger. In his concussed state, Wyatt must have thought

Mike was Cash. Laura gently patted Mike's arm, grateful she had the distraction of comforting the older man to keep her focus off the way her heart was racing.

At least Wyatt was conscious.

A good sign, but he wasn't out of the woods.

Laura longed to go to Wyatt and hold his hand, but she knew she'd be in the way of the paramedics doing their job.

She had to stay strong.

"Nothing to be sorry about," Mike said. "Just focus on what the doctors tell you, and you'll be fine."

Wyatt struggled against the restraints. "No. You have to know I'm sorry. Please forgive me. I didn't mean to kill you. I can't keep living with the guilt. Tell me you forgive me."

The desperation in Wyatt's voice made tears well in Laura's eyes. Poor Wyatt. Clearly he'd been hit hard, to think he'd killed Cash. Cash had been alone in the car when he'd died. Wyatt had nothing to do with it.

"What is he talking about?" Barbara asked, stepping in to the group, Garrett in her arms.

"It's just the concussion talking," Laura said.

"I need you all to step back," the paramedic said. "We've got to get him to the hospital."

They did as he asked, and Laura turned to the Fishers. "I need to be with my husband. Can you and Abigail take the boys back to the hotel? I'll be in touch as soon as I have information to share."

"Of course," Mike said.

Tony joined their group. "You can borrow my truck to get to the hospital so they have the baby stuff from your truck," he said. "Don't worry about what he said about killing Cash. People say and do strange things when they have a concussion. Last one I had, I was convinced that my nurse was my ex-wife, and boy, did that not go over well."

Though Laura knew Tony was trying to make her feel better, it didn't ease the worry in her heart. Cash had died as a result of an untreated concussion. And while Laura wasn't going to let Wyatt behind the wheel anytime soon, the similarity plagued her.

Her throat clogged with emotion, she nodded at Tony, then turned her attention to the only One who could help.

Please, God, she prayed. *Don't let me lose another husband.*

Wyatt drifted in and out of consciousness, and when he finally came to, all he could think about was Cash. He remembered at some point, asking Cash for forgiveness for killing him, but now that he was awake in the hospital, he felt overwhelmed with grief.

Cash was dead, but Wyatt was alive.

A nurse came in and checked on him. "How are you feeling?"

Wyatt blinked at her. He'd had enough concussions to know this was standard operating procedure. She'd ask him a bunch of questions to see how much damage he'd sustained cognitively.

But that was the problem. The damage was to his heart, not his brain.

As if to rub in his pain, Laura was on the other side of the bed, and she squeezed his hand. "You're going to be okay. You haven't been unconscious that long, and preliminary tests don't show any bleeding in the brain."

"We still have more tests to do now that he's awake," the nurse said.

Tests. Wyatt closed his eyes again. He was too tired for tests. Besides, there weren't tests to diagnose what was really wrong with him. Not that he needed them. He already knew. The weight of the guilt of killing his best friend was too strong.

He'd thought it would be enough to take

care of Laura and the boys, that it would somehow make up for his sins. But he'd been wrong.

When he got on that bronc, he looked over at where Laura always sat, and he felt the weight of Barbara's eyes on him.

Last night had been a terrible reminder of everything he'd taken from Cash. The beautiful wife, the children, even his standing as one of the top bareback bronc riders in the world. All things Barbara had pointed out.

His chest hurt as he thought about it all. He didn't deserve for those boys to call him Daddy, yet he was the one who'd started it. Laura had encouraged it, because she encouraged him in everything, just like she was doing now.

"Wyatt? Can you stay awake to answer the nurse's questions?" Laura's sweet voice tried to bring him back, but he couldn't open his eyes and face her.

He'd thought that marrying her and taking care of the boys was the honorable thing to do, but that kiss made him realize how foolish he'd been. He wanted Laura for himself, and as much as he tried to justify it, it felt like he'd killed his friend to take over his life.

Just like Barbara's eyes had accused him of doing.

"Wyatt, please," Laura said as she squeezed his hand. "We need you. I need you."

Poor, sweet, innocent Laura. She believed in him because she didn't know the truth. Had Laura been there when he'd confessed to killing Cash? He remembered saying something, and arguing with the paramedic over it. He'd been trying to tell everyone he killed Cash, and the paramedic telling him he didn't kill anyone, he just had a bad head injury.

Now it was time to set the record straight.

All this time, he'd lived in fear of his secret being revealed. But now he knew the weight of it was too much to bear.

Wyatt opened his eyes and looked at his wife. "I killed Cash," he said.

Laura gave him a sympathetic look, then turned her attention to the nurse. "He's been saying that since he got injured. Which makes no sense, since Cash died in a car accident. I'm not sure what part of the brain it means he injured, but you should schedule whatever tests are needed to check it out."

"No!" Wyatt strained against the wires and things attached to him and tried to sit up. "I killed him. Cash is dead because of me."

The nurse pushed him down. "You need to lie still." Then she pushed the call button. "I need some help in here, restraining a patient with a head injury."

"It's going to be okay," Laura told him.

He could tell she was trying to calm him down, but he didn't want or need to be calmed down.

"Listen to me," Wyatt said. "Cash is dead because of me."

Laura rubbed his arm gently. "Okay. Lie back down and rest. Tell me why you think you killed Cash."

She looked up at the nurse, and Wyatt knew what she was doing. He'd done the same thing with other friends with concussions. You tell them what they want to hear so they'll calm down and the doctors could do their work. Fine. But before they filled him with whatever drugs they used to make him rest, he was going to tell the truth.

"I knew he had a concussion that day. He wasn't fit to drive, and I let him get in his truck and drive off. Instead, I was more worried about meeting with some potential sponsors, which is why I'd driven myself."

"But you don't have sponsors," Laura said quietly.

Was she really that dense? Wyatt tried turning to look over at her, but the thing they had his neck in made it almost impossible.

"I turned it down," Wyatt said. "How could I have accepted a deal where I'd been too focused on myself to worry about a friend who needed me? I should have been there for Cash. I should have insisted he get medical treatment for his concussion, and I shouldn't have let him get into the truck. His blood was all over that money, and I couldn't take it."

Instead of getting angry, Laura only looked sympathetic. "That's a lot of shoulds, when we both know how stubborn Cash was. Rest now, and once you're in a better frame of mind, we'll talk it out. Maybe find someone who can help you sort through the guilt you feel over Cash's death."

Wyatt closed his eyes again. She didn't get it, because she hadn't been there. Hadn't seen the way Cash staggered. Hadn't had that niggling feeling in the back of his mind that something was seriously wrong with his friend.

No talking could fix what he had done.

The door to his room opened, and more medical people came in. He'd be busy with tests and them poking and prodding him to make sure he was going to be okay. All the things Cash had needed and Wyatt hadn't gotten for him.

One more thing Wyatt had stolen from his friend.

But he could make part of it right. He had to stop profiting from his friend's death.

He opened his eyes and looked at Laura.

"I want an annulment," he said.

Chapter Ten

An annulment?

Laura couldn't have heard Wyatt right, but then he turned to the nurse on the other side of him. "I don't want her here."

"Wyatt..." Laura said, trying to understand what her husband was saying. Clearly this head injury had hurt him more than she'd realized.

"Get. Out." Wyatt's voice was harsher than she'd ever heard him say anything.

"I don't understand." Laura was trying not to cry, because she had to be strong for him. But how was she supposed to be strong, when he was kicking her out?

Wyatt strained to sit up again.

"GET OUT!" he yelled, and the crew of nurses worked to restrain him.

The nurse who'd been with Wyatt the whole time came to Laura's side. "Sometimes head injury patients get combative with their loved ones. This is all perfectly normal. But we need to get him stabilized, and since your presence is upsetting to him, I'm going to have to ask you to leave until we do."

Laura nodded slowly. All she'd wanted was to be here for Wyatt, and instead, she was making things worse.

"Of course. Whatever you think is best."

When she went out into the hall, the doctor came with her. "I'm sorry you had to go through that," she said. "We'll do our best to calm him down and get him stable, so until then, I just need you to sit tight and wait."

Trying not to cry, Laura said, "I just need to know he's going to be okay."

The doctor smiled at her. "He'll live. But until we get through all the tests, I don't know where he'll be cognitively. It's going to take time, so just be patient."

Gesturing at the waiting area, the doctor continued. "It may be a while, so even though you're welcome to hang out there, you might think about getting something to eat, or maybe going home and taking a shower. We've got your contact information and I'll have the staff get in touch as soon as he's able to have you with him."

Laura walked over to the waiting area she'd been shown when they'd first admitted Wyatt in to the hospital. It had been hours, and this break would give her some time to check in with the Fishers and see how the boys were doing.

When she called Barbara, it went straight to voice mail. She tried Mike. Voice mail again. Strange.

Abigail picked up immediately. "Hey. How's Wyatt?"

"Okay. I'll tell you about it in a minute. I was just calling to check on the boys. Mike and Barbara aren't answering their phones."

"Oh," Abigail said. "The boys were cranky and Barbara was upset, so Mike took them all back to the hotel to rest. I stayed behind to gather everyone's things. Gracie was going to help me get Wyatt's gear back together, but she got pulled into that interview with the Rodeo Network people, so I'm just waiting for her."

Laura took a deep breath. "So they're probably all napping."

"Probably," Abigail said. "They were all exhausted, and Mike seemed pretty upset. It had to be hard on him, seeing Wyatt injured and saying all that weird stuff about Cash. So how is Wyatt?"

She quickly shared what was going on with Wyatt—except his annulment request—trying to sound positive, but Laura's stomach started to feel sick. What if everything wasn't going to be fine? Some people's personalities completely changed as a result of having a head injury. What if Wyatt was being serious about the annulment?

But now was not the time to give in to the panic and fear, despite her racing heart. Laura had other obligations, and as much as she wanted to figure things out with Wyatt, she had to be strong for the sake of her boys.

"What can I do to help?" Abigail asked. "I'm kind of stuck at the rodeo because I gave the keys to your truck to the Fishers so they could move the car seat bases to theirs, but they forgot to bring them back to me. Gracie said she'd take me to the hotel when she was done, but who knows how long that will be."

Especially since Gracie took forever to do things. Laura loved her friend, but she also knew that getting out of anywhere with Gracie was next to impossible, because Gracie knew everyone and had to stop and have long conversations with them. Harvey joked that it took her two hours to get a gallon of milk because everyone at the store was her best friend.

Laura glanced at her phone. Though the boys were probably fine, with all this emotional upheaval what she really needed most right now was a quick cuddle. It bothered her that the Fishers weren't answering their phones, nap or not.

The thought of taking care of her children was the only thing keeping Laura grounded right now, and she would feel a lot better once they were in her arms.

"I have Tony's truck, so I can come pick you up. We'll go back to the hotel to check on the boys, then I can get my truck keys from the Fishers and figure out the vehicle situation. Hopefully by then, they'll have Wyatt in a place where I can be with him again."

They made a few final arrangements, and Laura stopped at the nurses' station to let them know what was going on. Once again, Laura thanked God for having such an incredible support system to make this all happen.

When she arrived at the rodeo, she found

Tony talking to Mark Mitchell, the rodeo doctor.

"How's Wyatt?" Mark asked.

Laura filled him in. As Mark nodded at what Laura shared, she realized that Mark might be able to shed some light on what happened with Cash's death.

"I know this is a weird question, but maybe you can help. Wyatt keeps saying that Cash's death is his fault. That he killed Cash. He blames himself for letting Cash drive with a concussion. Can you shed any light on to that?"

Mark ran his hand over his face. "It didn't occur to me that Wyatt would blame himself. If anyone is to blame, it's me. I examined Cash after his fall. He passed all the tests. He was shook up, but I didn't see anything that made me think he needed medical attention. Cash said he felt fine, but Wyatt was bugging him to get checked out. Ultimately, I agreed with Cash."

The look of grief on the man's face made Laura's heart ache.

"I keep asking myself if there's something I missed, something I should have done differently. But as I read through my notes and replay everything that happened that day, I can't see anything that would have made me change things."

Laura reached forward and hugged the man. "It's not your fault. I know this is painful for you, but when Wyatt is up to it, would you be willing to tell him this? Maybe it would help him stop blaming himself for Cash's death."

"Of course. I'm so sorry that you've gone through all this. I'm happy to help in any way I can."

As she turned to leave, Mark stopped her. "There is one more thing about the day Cash died. He was more upset than usual about having lost. He kept muttering about not knowing how he was going to get the money, but when I asked him about it, he waved me off, saying it wasn't my problem. I don't know if that helps or not, but that's what we talked about during my exam. He didn't seem physically hurt, just really stressed."

Unfortunately, it made too much sense. Laura smiled at the doctor. "Thank you, it actually helps a lot."

What Wyatt had thought was Cash dealing with the effects of a concussion was actually him realizing that he owed some really bad men a lot of money and had no means to repay them. And, after what the men had done to their home, Laura could see where Cash was absolutely terrified.

She briefly explained the vehicle situation to Tony, who agreed to help with transportation as they sorted out getting the keys to her truck, then coming back here for it. So many complications, but she felt supported in all of it.

When they got back to the hotel, Laura knew something was wrong. The Fishers hadn't been to the room. Everything was exactly where Laura had left it when she'd gone out that morning, down to the formula she'd accidentally spilled on the counter when making the boys' bottles.

Another call to both of them went to voice mail.

Where were they?

Laura's head started pounding in unison with her heart.

"I think we should call the police," Abigail said.

Tony nodded. "I hate to agree with her, but they were acting funny after you left the rodeo. I thought they were just upset about Wyatt and what he said, but is there a chance they simply took the boys?"

Laura wanted to throw up as she realized all the things she'd overlooked, trying to be supportive of Cash's parents, their grief and her desire for them to have a relationship with the twins despite everything they'd put her through.

Tears streamed down her face as she finally allowed herself to cry over what a mess this day had been.

First her husband had been injured and didn't want anything to do with her, and now her boys were missing.

All day long, she'd done nothing but praise and thank God for her many blessings. But where were her blessings now?

She wanted to scream and cry, but words failed her as she tried to ask God for help. Throat clogged with the tears she hadn't allowed herself to cry, she wouldn't have been able to speak even if she had the words to express her feelings at every unthinkable tragedy hitting at once.

Wyatt stared blankly at the television in his hospital room. The medical staff had finally left him in peace, but there was no peace in his heart.

Telling Laura to leave and asking for an annulment had been the right thing to do for her sake. She deserved better than a man like him.

But it didn't mean he didn't feel like his heart had been ripped out.

Once they deemed him medically sound, he'd call his lawyer and arrange for the annulment, as well as sufficient funds to take care of Laura and the boys. That's all this marriage had been about anyway.

That, and protecting her from the Fishers, but she had her family for that.

His phone buzzed, and Wyatt grabbed it to shut it off. He thought he'd put it on Do Not Disturb so no one would bother him, but he must have done it wrong.

As he glanced at the message, he did a double take, and his heart sank.

It was an Amber Alert.

For his boys.

His breath came fast as Wyatt ripped out the wires on him, making all the alarms go off. His head still pounded from the blow he'd taken earlier, but it didn't matter.

Nothing mattered.

Other than finding his boys.

One of the nurses came rushing in. "Sir! We told you not to touch those. You're going to hurt yourself."

He held up his phone. "Do you see this?"

The nurse barely glanced at it. "Yes, it's an Amber Alert. All of our phones are going crazy with it."

"Those are my children," Wyatt said. "Now you need to get me unhooked from all this nonsense so I can find my boys."

"Sir, I'm afraid we can't do that."

Wyatt pointed to the IV in his arm. "Get this thing out of me or I'll do it myself. Then you'll have a lot of blood and stuff to clean up, and I'm sure you don't want to deal with that mess."

The nurse hesitated.

"My children have been kidnapped," Wyatt said, raising his voice.

More of the medical staff came into the room.

"Good. One of you needs to get me out of this mess so I can help find my sons."

The nurse glanced back at the people who'd just entered the room. "He seems to think that Amber Alert is about his children."

"It is." Tony strode into the room, flanked by a police officer. "Now, I'm not opposed to you keeping him in here if this is where he needs to be, but if you're going to restrain him or give him knockout drugs, I need information from him first."

Wyatt felt ridiculous, standing in front of his friend in a hospital gown with those weird nonslip socks on, everyone at the ready to take him on. Though what he wanted most was to find his boys, he knew these people weren't going to let him leave without a fight.

He sank back against his bed, feeling more helpless than he had in his entire life. "What can I do to help?"

"Laura asked the Fishers to watch the boys while she came with you to the hospital. It looks like they've kidnapped them instead. The police have already checked their house, and they aren't there. Do you have any idea where they might have taken them?"

One more thing that was his fault. All he'd wanted was to help Laura, and yet, because of how he'd made the Fishers feel threatened, they'd kidnapped his boys. No, her boys. It wasn't fair for him to call them his anymore.

Closing his eyes, Wyatt tried to think of anything that might help the police find the boys. Poor Laura. He'd tried so hard to do the right thing by her, but it seemed like he just kept messing things up.

Finally, a memory hit him, and he said, "Did you check the lake house? It belonged to Barbara's sister, but I think when she passed away, Barbara got it. It's hard to get to, and out of the way, so it would be a good place for them to hide out."

"Can you give us the address?" the police officer asked.

Wyatt shook his head. "No clue. It wouldn't help anyway. GPS is always wrong about the directions, and there aren't any street signs. It's pretty rustic. I know how to get there, though."

"No," Tony said. "Laura would be furious if you left the hospital before you were ready. She's worried enough about the boys. Don't make her worry about you, too."

His heart ached at the thought of what Laura must be going through. Part of him wished he could be there for her, but he'd already messed up her life enough as it was. At least she had her sister.

Living with the pain of what he'd already done was unbearable to Wyatt, but if something happened to the twins, he wasn't sure he could live with himself.

"Please," Wyatt said. "It's hard to find, and there's no cell service out there. Let me do this."

He looked over at the doctor. "You said you were just keeping me for observation. You said you were concerned about how upset I keep getting. Can you see where I might have reason to be upset? Do you think I'm going to get any rest, knowing my children are missing?"

The expression on the doctor's face told him he'd won. Though it usually took forever to get out of a hospital, with the police officer standing there impatiently, they let him go in record time.

When they reached the parking lot, Laura was waiting with another police officer. Tony turned to him. "I can have someone pick me up so she can ride with you to the lake house."

"No," Wyatt said. "I can't face her right now."

Tony looked disgusted with him. "Unbelievable. Her babies are missing, and you're too busy beating yourself up over the past to be there for her in the present. I never realized what a jerk you were until now."

Not waiting for Wyatt's response, Tony strode over to Laura and talked to her. Though Wyatt couldn't hear what they were saying, he could tell by her body language that she was upset.

He'd deal with that later. For now, finding the boys was the most important thing.

Despite Wyatt's desire not to face her, Laura had other ideas. She came over and got into the police car with him. "The officer said I should ride in here," she said.

"Fine."

He turned and looked out the window.

"I thought the boys would be safe with them," Laura said, her voice sounding clogged with tears. "I'm so sorry. I never imagined they'd stoop so low."

She started crying, and as much as Wyatt had promised himself he was going to let her go, he couldn't let her go like this.

Wyatt leaned over and put his arm around her. "It's not your fault. It's mine."

That small confession eased some of the pain in his heart. It felt good to finally be honest with her.

"It's no one's fault," the police officer said. "People take babies all the time, even people you trust. You can't blame yourselves. Instead, we have to focus our energy on getting them back. They can't have gotten far, and with the Amber Alert, everyone is looking for them."

Laura snuggled up to him, and as much as it felt good to have her in his arms, he couldn't let her think anything had changed between them.

"I'm so glad you're going to be okay," she said.

"Don't." He pulled his arm away and looked at her. "This doesn't change the fact that you deserve better than I can give you. It's not fair that I've taken so much from you."

"So you would take my heart, too?" More tears rolled down her face, and he hated that he was the cause.

"Don't talk like that," he said.

Laura straightened and brushed the tears from her face. "Don't tell me what to do. My babies are missing, and you think that this is the right time to stomp on my heart even more?"

The she leaned forward. "Officer, I'm sorry for what you're about to hear, but this idiot needs a few truth bombs before he messes up our lives even more than he already has."

Instead of looking concerned, the police officer smiled gently. "You go right ahead. If someone took my babies, I'd be dropping a whole lot of truth bombs myself."

Though Wyatt had stared down his share of angry broncs, and even a few riled-up bulls, nothing had prepared him for the look on Laura's face.

"Cash's death was not your fault," she said. "I talked to the rodeo doctor myself. He examined Cash before he left. Cash wasn't hurt. He was upset at losing because he had no way to repay those loan sharks that visited me."

Wyatt closed his eyes and leaned back against the seat. Cash had lost. He'd forgotten that fact. Failed to make the connection between that and the visit from the Chapman brothers.

"He listened to you. After you told him to, Cash saw the doctor, and the doctor said he passed all the tests."

Which Wyatt wouldn't have known because he was having dinner with the potential sponsors.

"But I still should have been there for him," Wyatt said. He should have realized how upset Cash was at losing and known something was wrong.

"How?" Laura asked. "How many times have we all laughed about how stubborn Cash was? Maybe you need to accept what the rest of us have all come to terms with. It was a tragic accident, and Cash is gone. And we need to do our best to continue living without him."

Wyatt's heart tore in two as he thought

back to that night. All the ways he'd questioned himself. Could what Laura said be true? He'd been blaming himself for not forcing Cash to see a doctor. But Cash had. And he'd been released.

"I still feel guilty that I have everything that was once Cash's," Wyatt finally said. "Barbara saw it, and I saw how she looked at me for it. It's my fault they took the boys."

He looked at Laura, trying to get her to understand how much culpability he had in this situation.

"No," Laura said. "Sure, the rodeo gave them the opportunity, but when we went to their house looking for the boys, it was very clear the place was set up for the babies to live with them. When I look back at everything, including the social services report, I can see where they weren't going to stop until they had my sons."

Their lawyer had suggested that had been the reason they'd filed the report with social services. No judge would give a child to the grandparents over a parent, but if they had proof of abuse, it made it easier for them to do so.

"It doesn't change the fact that I have everything that was once Cash's. I feel like I've stolen it from him. I thought I was doing what he asked, taking care of you and the boys. But I fell in love and messed it all up."

The words slipped out before he could take them back.

Laura reached over and took his hand. "I fell in love, too. So rather than fighting this and making excuses, why don't we do what we promised each other that day in the truck, and communicate? Let's figure this out together. After we find out sons."

This time, when Wyatt closed his eyes, he asked for God's wisdom, instead of relying on what he'd thought were facts. If he'd been wrong all this time about his role in Cash's death, could he be wrong about other things as well?

"We've reached the lake area," the police officer said.

Thankful for a break from his conflicting emotions, Wyatt directed him through the maze of dirt roads leading to the cabin.

When they arrived there, the Fishers' truck was parked out front.

As Laura sat in the police cruiser, holding her babies, tears streamed down her face. Thankfully, the Fishers gave up the boys without issue, and it seemed almost anticlimactic to watch them being led in handcuffs to the police car.

"Those are my grandchildren," Barbara screamed. "I have every right to see them. Don't take them away the way my son was taken from me."

The grief in the older woman's voice tore at Laura's heart. She'd overheard the police officer interviewing Mike, who claimed that he was just trying to help Barbara get through her grief and they'd never intended to keep the boys forever. He'd thought Laura wouldn't notice or mind if they kept them for a few days while she dealt with Wyatt being in the hospital.

In a way, Mike had argued, they were helping her so she had one less thing to worry about.

Which Laura would have almost bought, except for the fact that they hadn't told her their plans.

The sad thing was, had they just communicated with her, this wouldn't have been a big deal. After all, she'd already asked them to watch the twins while she was at the hospital. Had they only done the right thing, they'd have been able to build some trust so that at some point, she'd have been open to letting them have more time with the boys.

Barbara had ranted about how Laura was an unfit mother, citing things like the broken porta crib and bringing the boys to the rodeo as proof that she couldn't take care of her own children.

In the past, those words would have bothered Laura. Laura would have taken it far more personally. But she would never be the same kind of mother Barbara was, and why would she want to be?

Cash had been so afraid of letting his mother down by not being the perfect son that he'd kept so many secrets from the people who loved him, not wanting to let them down. Their life could have been so different had he simply confessed to Laura what was going on.

She glanced over to where Wyatt was talking to a police officer. The question was, would Wyatt be willing to learn from that mistake and move forward in their relationship?

She'd confessed her love to him, and asked him if he was willing to figure things out, but in the hours since then, they'd been consumed with making sure the babies were okay and dealing with the fallout from the Fishers' actions.

Garrett wiggled in her grasp. The boys had been cooped up for longer than normal and they just wanted to be free. She'd probably been holding them a little too tightly as well. But how could she not? Even though they'd never been in any real danger, the fear of losing them had made her want to hold on all the more.

But as she glanced over at Barbara in the police car, Laura realized that was probably Barbara's problem. Holding on too tight.

Laura got out of the car, and carried the boys over to Wyatt. "Can you take one for me? They're getting antsy from being cooped up, and I can't handle both of them."

He looked like he was going to refuse, but then he said, "Come here, Gare-bear," and held out his arms.

Garrett immediately reached for the man he'd come to know as his father. Did Wyatt see that? It wasn't just Laura who'd fallen in love.

Having the baby in his arms seemed to lift Wyatt's mood. Wyatt clung to Garrett just as tightly as the little boy clung to him.

He'd held the boys briefly after they'd been rescued, but this was the first he'd really gotten quality time with them. Wyatt's heart was hurting, too, though he was being too stubborn to admit it.

"I'm sorry I've been hogging them," Laura said, trying to break the ice.

"They're your boys," he said. "It's your right."

The cold tone to his voice made her want to hold him just as tightly as she held her boys. "They're yours, too," she said.

"No. They're Cash's, and I made a mistake in trying to let them be mine."

"You're acting just like him, you know."

Wyatt glared at her. "Excuse me?"

"No, I won't. There are no excuses for how you're behaving right now. I realize you're recovering from a head injury. But I have countered every single one of your lame excuses for acting like a jerk, and rather than facing the truth, you're digging your heels in the way Cash did and refusing to face facts."

Cody giggled in her arms, and she smiled down at him. "Oh, you like it when Mommy tells off Daddy, do you? Maybe I should do it more often."

When she looked back at Wyatt, even he was smiling.

"Look, Wyatt, I get. Love is scary, especially when it comes with all the baggage we have. But having had love, even with the horrible way things ended for me, I can tell you that it's worth it. And we can have something even better if we're willing to fight for it."

As she spoke, his smile had turned back into a look of concern.

"But Cash—"

"Is dead. And it's not your fault. Cash's primary desire was for the people around him to be happy. That's why he hid his failings from all of us. He'd be the last person to stand in the way of our happiness. If he were standing here right now, he'd tell you to stop being a bonehead."

Wyatt laughed. "He did call me a bonehead a lot."

"That's because you are one." Laura smiled at him. "But I have faith in your ability to make things right. Cash would have wanted you to be happy, not to deny yourself out of some misguided sense of nobility."

Garrett reached up and grabbed Wyatt's face.

"Hey!" Wyatt said.

Laura laughed. "I think he's checking to see if you're a bonehead or not."

Laughing with her, Wyatt kissed the baby

on top of his head. "Okay, point taken. I'll stop being a bonehead."

"And that means?"

Wyatt looked down at the baby he held, then over at Laura. "I've been relying on my version of the truth for a long time. When you told me you loved me in the car, I decided to stop relying on my own understanding, and seek God's wisdom instead."

He gave Garrett a squeeze. "I love these guys so much it hurts. I was willing to give them up, if only for the sake of their happiness and well-being. But that's not what you asked. You asked me to figure it out. To work together, and solve our problems together. So, okay. Let's do this."

After adjusting the baby in his arms, Wyatt leaned forward and kissed Laura. The third time must have been the charm, because Laura felt the tingle all the way down to her toes, and despite them each having a squirmy baby in their arms, the boys let them kiss.

Maybe it was the twins' way of saying, "Finally. Mom and Dad are figuring it out."

Epilogue

Just over a year later, Laura sat in the stands at the world championships, cheering Wyatt on. He hadn't won the previous year, as that honor had gone to Harvey, which meant Gracie was sitting next to her, rubbing her pregnant belly in satisfaction. The boys were crashed in their stroller, exhausted from a long day of running around and being spoiled by their rodeo family. Bringing a pair of toddlers to the World Championship Rodeo was not for the faint of heart, and Laura wouldn't have been able to do it without the loving support of her friends and family.

Tomorrow, they'd be going to Texas to visit Barbara, who was serving out her sentence for kidnapping the boys. Though Laura had asked for leniency in the Fishers' case, they'd still been sentenced to jail for their actions. Thankfully, they had listened to Laura's plea for them to get mental help for Barbara, who was finally dealing with her grief over Cash's death. Mike was in another facility, and they'd visit him as well. Her correspondence with both Fishers had been positive, and Laura was hopeful that they could eventually establish a healthy family relationship.

Finally, it was Wyatt's turn. As she said her usual prayer, she watched as the bronc came shooting out of the gate. Beautifully. Brilliantly. As perfect as any ride Laura had ever seen. When the buzzer rang, it was clear to everyone in the stands that Wyatt had won. His score being announced was a mere formality in acknowledging that he'd had a great ride.

As the stands erupted in cheers, Gracie leaned over to Laura and said, "I guess it's your turn for a baby. Hope you're ready for another one."

Laura smiled, placed a hand on her own belly and whispered to her friend, "Since I'm already expecting, I guess it's a good thing Wyatt won."

"What?" Gracie squealed and hugged Laura tight.

"Shh...we haven't told a lot of people yet. Come on—let's go find our husbands."

Gracie gave her another hug. "Oh, I hope it's a girl. That way, my little girl will have a built-in bestie."

Laughing, Laura said, "We're hoping for another boy. Wyatt has his heart set on naming him Cash. But all that really matters is that it's healthy."

She adjusted the still sleeping boys in their stroller and started for the area where she could meet up with Wyatt. How they could sleep through this ruckus, she didn't know, but at least they were content.

Though Laura had asked Gracie to keep it quiet about the baby, Gracie pattered on about how either way, her baby would have a best friend or a husband. But Laura was too happy to discourage her rambling.

Waiting in the wings, Laura watched her husband accept congratulations from other competitors as well as get interviewed by the Rodeo Network staff. Wyatt had finally won the world championship. He broke free from the crowd and came to her, picking her up as he always did, before swinging her around and giving her a kiss.

Laura had once told him she didn't need

the fairy tale. But married to Wyatt, who was committed to working through things with her, she had something better.

* * * * *

If you enjoyed this Shepherd's Creek book by Danica Favorite, be sure to pick up the previous book in this series:

Journey to Forgiveness

Available now from Love Inspired!

Dear Reader,

Every time I finish a book, I'm overwhelmed at the work God did in me while writing it. So I pray, for anyone in a grieving season, that God will bring you the comfort and healing you need.

I enjoyed writing about the rodeo aspect, since I've spent so much of my life around rodeos. I would be remiss if I didn't tell you that I intentionally changed some details, like network and rodeo names. When I started writing this book, I was sitting on my couch, watching my daughter perform at a rodeo being broadcast on television. Of course, I watched all the other events, including the one featured in this book, bareback bronc riding. As soon as I finish writing this, I'll be online, booking hotels for the rodeos we'll be at this summer. If you've never been to a rodeo, I highly encourage you to check one out.

Until then, be sure to follow me online, where I'll probably post way too many pictures of all the horse activities we're involved in. You can find all my contact information at DanicaFavorite.com.

May you find yourself richly blessed by God,
Danica Favorite

COMING NEXT MONTH FROM
Love Inspired

PINECRAFT REFUGE
Pinecraft Seasons • by Lenora Worth

Grieving widower Tanner Dawson has no intentions of ever marrying again, but when he meets Eva Miller sparks fly. Giving her a job at his store is the last thing he wants, but he needs the help. As they get closer, can he keep his secrets to protect his daughter?

THE SECRET AMISH ADMIRER
by Virginia Wise

Shy Eliza Zook has secretly been in love with popular Gabriel King since they were children, but he has never noticed her. When a farm injury forces Gabriel to work alongside her in an Amish gift shop, will it be her chance to finally win him over?

REUNITED BY THE BABY
Sunset Ridge • by Brenda Minton

After finding a baby abandoned in the back of his truck, Matthew Rivers enlists the help of RN Parker Smythe, the woman whose love he once rejected. When their feelings start to blossom, could it lead them on a path to something more?

HER ALASKAN RETURN
Serenity Peak • by Belle Calhoune

Back in her hometown in Alaska, single and pregnant Autumn Hines comes face-to-face with first love Judah Campbell when her truck breaks down. Still reeling from tragedy, the widowed fisherman finds hope when he reconnects with Autumn. But can their relationship withstand the secret she's been keeping?

A HOME FOR THE TWINS
by Danielle Thorne

The struggling Azalea Inn is the perfect spot for chef Lindsey Judd to raise her twin boys. But things get complicated when lawyer Donovan Ainsworth comes to stay. Love is the last thing either of them want, but two little matchmakers might feel differently...

HIS TEMPORARY FAMILY
by Julie Brookman

Firefighter Sam Tiernan's life gets turned upside down when a car accident leaves his baby nieces in his care. When his matchmaking grandmother ropes next-door neighbor Fiona Shay into helping him, it might be the push they both need to open their hearts to something more...
